POISON

Mysteries by Alane Ferguson:

OVERKILL

SHOW ME THE EVIDENCE
An Edgar Allan Poe Award–winner

POISON

by ALANE FERGUSON

Bradbury Press • New York

Maxwell Macmillan Canada Toronto
Maxwell Macmillan International
New York Oxford Singapore Sydney

7840

Bradbury Press
Macmillan Publishing Company
866 Third Avenue
New York, NY 10022

Maxwell Macmillan Canada, Inc.
1200 Eglinton Avenue East
Suite 200
Don Mills, Ontario M3C 3N1

Macmillan Publishing Company is part of the Maxwell
Communication Group of Companies.
First edition
Printed and bound in the United States of America
Printed on acid-free paper
10 9 8 7 6 5 4 3 2 1
The text of this book is set in 12-point Caledonia.

LIBRARY OF CONGRESS CATALOGING-IN-PUBLICATION DATA
Ferguson, Alane.
Poison / by Alane Ferguson. — 1st ed.
p.   cm.
Summary: Following the mysterious death of her stepmother, Chelsea and her
best friend, Amber, attempt to snare the killer, but instead find themselves
wrapped up in a dangerous game of cat and mouse.
ISBN 0-02-734528-9
[1. Mystery and detective stories.]   I. Title.
PZ7.F3547Po   1994
[Fic]—dc20   94-10560

To Serena Rose Nolan,
the sister who warms my life
with her music and love

A special thanks to Ellen Reddick
for her generous help

POISON

1

"So then he goes, 'No way!' and I go, 'Way!' and then I just laughed. I couldn't *believe* it!"

"Umm-humm," Chelsea murmured. She pressed the phone to her ear and glanced over her shoulder. The door to her father's office was tightly shut, so there was no way for him to know that she was making still another personal call. He'd forbidden her to talk to Amber on company time, but so what? Chelsea knew that now more than ever she needed to connect to someone, even if it was merely through the umbilical cord of the telephone.

"Well, anyway, I really miss you, Chelsea. It's been forever!" Amber sighed. Her voice was almost drowned out by the squeal and ka-thunk of a swimmer doing a cannonball.

"I miss you, too. I miss all you guys. And I *really* miss your pool!"

"Thanks a lot. I was wondering why you suddenly turned up again, and I guess that about explains it. And even though that comment was unbelievably tacky, I still say it would be more fun if you were here. So sneak out and come over."

"I can't. You have some fun for me."

Chelsea pictured Amber and her friends, roasting to perfection in the June sun while she, Chelsea, was forced to grind away her summer in her dad's office. She could almost smell the sweet scent of the suntan lotion over the phone, could almost feel the cold droplets baking off her arms and legs until her skin tightened like the head of a drum. Amber and Brett and Jimmy and Vanessa were all there, splayed on the concrete. Listening to the mix of water splashing and radio and poolside conversation, Chelsea tried to dismiss a stab of envy.

Amber seemed to sense her thoughts, because suddenly she chirped, "Listen, there's been an amazing amount of activity in the guy department since you decided to socialize with us again. They're all asking."

"Yeah. Right." Shaking her head, Chelsea smiled into the phone.

"It's true! Every guy has asked me when *you're* going to quit work and come play. *I'm* here, which, of course, counts for nothing. They want *you*. I can't decide if it's 'cause you're skinny, or because you're blond—"

Snorting, Chelsea said, "Give me a break—"

"No! Really! It's got to be one of those two things. Skinny, or blond. So I've decided to send you chocolate on the principle that it'll be a lot easier to make you fat than me thin. The only problem left will be how to make you short. And brunette. Of course, you used to be sort of darker until you started the bleach habit and you became dependent on the bottle."

Chelsea shook her head and grinned. It was good to talk on the phone, to act as if her life hadn't changed, as if nothing had happened and she was the same person she'd been before. *Just laugh with Amber and pretend.*

"I only lightened my hair one shade," she said. "It's a color *weave*."

"It's an unfair advantage. You have to play fair."

"Listen, Amber, I'd love to take the time to explain how bizarre you are, but I've got to go."

"No! We just got started! We never get to talk. Remember that one time when we argued over the phone until one o'clock in the morning? Remember that?"

"No . . ."

"Last year. When you said you thought trees had souls and people who cut them down were guilty of murder, and I said if you'd damn the souls of lumberjacks for the murder of trees then you should run around buck naked because you'd killed a million cotton plants and at least one cow, and you said, 'Fine, I'll start if you do.'"

"I never said that."

"Yes you did. It was at the height of your environmental phase. We never get to talk like that anymore. And nobody else in the whole world can talk like you do, Chelsea."

Looking over her shoulder once again, Chelsea hunched over the phone and dropped her voice. "I'm sorry, but Dad's secretary could be back any minute, and I can hear him stomping around his office right now. If either one of them catches me on the phone, I'll be toast." Touching the receiver in a tiny salute, Chelsea added, "He's given me orders."

"He's really not going to let you out of there?"

"No."

Although she couldn't see Amber over the phone, Chelsea could tell she was biting her lip. "I can't believe he just drafted you, like you're in the army or something. Do you realize that this is the only summer that you'll be seventeen—and you're locked away at Smythe Towers! I've hardly seen you all year. I kept thinking we'd get together in the summer, and now this. It's just not fair!"

"Well, who told you life was fair? Especially *my* life?" Trying to keep an edge from creeping into her voice, Chelsea added, "My dad said I have to be his receptionist. He says I have to learn the value of *work*. You know I can't argue with him." Stabbing her pen into the edge of the blotter hard enough to leave a small hole, she added, "I'm serving time. It's just the way it is."

When she didn't say more, Chelsea heard a flutter of laughter. "Well, anyway, Smythe Towers is so gorgeous—it's hardly like you're stuck flipping burgers. It must be like working on the set of Star Trek."

With a jagged motion, Chelsea added a mirage under the ragged edges of the palm trees she'd been doodling since Amber called. Of course, her father's building was breathtaking. Above her, a vaulted, sky-lighted ceiling filtered the sun. Stark shapes of New Age sculpture shadowed massive walls of pale stone. Geometric paintings seemed to bleed color against the sand-colored walls, and carefully polished plants grew in chrome cylinders that reminded Chelsea of bullets.

It was a beautiful prison.

She glanced over her shoulder at her father's office. "Listen, Amber, I'm going to have to let you go. I have a feeling I'm going to get busted, so—" She was about to finish with good-bye, when she heard a shift in Amber's tone.

"Wait. Can I ask you something? It's . . . important."

"Okay. But be quick."

"Is your—" Her voice shifted again. "No, maybe I should bring it up in person. Forget it."

Typical Amber, Chelsea thought. In the five years she'd known her, Amber would always repeat the same pattern: start light, make you laugh, then hit with something a little harder. It seemed as if she needed to warm up the audience before getting to the punch line.

"Just ask, Amber. Please."

"Okay." Amber seemed to be weighing her next few words. Finally, she said, "My mom was supposed to have lunch with Diane today, and Diane didn't show. They're on that symphony committee together, you know? And she never even called to break the date."

"Diane has stood people up before," Chelsea said, her voice cold. "I'm sorry. It's just . . . her. Besides, I'm out of the loop. What she does, she does."

"But, my point is, I think it's weird the way she seems to have just dropped out of everything. Have you heard anything from her at all? Since she left, I mean?"

"No. And I told you before that I don't want to talk about it."

"I realize that, but since no one's even spoken with her, it occurred to me that Diane might be hurt or something and—"

"Excuse me, but I *said* I don't want to talk about it. Diane is fine. So just stop, okay?"

Chelsea was surprised that the mention of her stepmother could still cause hurt, anger, and fear to curl together like a braid of smoke. Hurt that Diane had just left Chelsea's life without any explanation. Anger when Chelsea found herself watching the phone, day after day, hoping to hear Diane's throaty voice across the wire. And fear when she realized that Diane could simply walk away.

Diane had been there eighteen mornings ago, smoothing panty hose over thin, muscled legs, and then she was gone. Three days after she'd left, Chelsea had drifted into Diane's bedroom to see if she could find some reason, some clue. Nothing had been moved, not any of the crisp clothes that hung in the large walk-in closet. Her shoes remained in hollow military rows, and the smell of her perfume—Poison—still clung to the fabric of her Donna Karan suits. Chelsea's fingertips had moved over the sable makeup brushes on Diane's vanity, touched the coolness of the gold metal lipstick cases and the velvet smoothness of her powder puff. Everything had been left exactly as if Diane would reappear and fall right back in step with their lives.

Just then, her father had walked past, looked in, then moved grimly on. The next day, everything of Diane's was packed and gone. Her father seemed bent on rubbing out every trace of his second wife.

"Well," Amber said now. Chelsea could tell she'd been stung. "I should let you go. Call me when you can."

Distant brays of laughter popped through the steady buzz of Amber's cordless phone.

"Look, I'm sorry, Amber."

"It's okay, Chels."

"Really, I know I'm raggy. It's been kind of tense lately. But I shouldn't snap at you."

"Forget it. I understand."

"Diane will call me as soon as she can," Chelsea said deliberately. "I'll just have to wait until she's ready."

"Can I ask you one more thing, or will I pull back a bloody stump?" Amber's tone was easy. Chelsea knew she'd been forgiven.

"Go ahead. Ask."

9

"I just wondered if your dad has explained what happened?"

"Something bad went down between them and Diane left. That's his entire version. I'm dying to talk to Diane myself, but I can't even find out where she lives now. I have to keep telling myself that Diane knows where I am, so the next move is hers."

Amber was quiet for a moment. In the past, they'd both been contented with moments of silence, but now, Chelsea was unsure of the rhythms. Fingering shiny dark leaves of periwinkle sprouting from a clay pot that Diane had given her, Chelsea let her mind drift. "Periwinkles are my kind of flower," Diane had said, setting the pot on the window ledge in Chelsea's bedroom. "Other people treat them like weeds, but I think they're perfect. They can take over any garden and bloom where they want because they demand their own space. And once they take root, no one—no one—can get rid of them."

"So what are you going to do?" Amber asked, breaking into her thoughts. "What's your next move?"

"I don't know. I've called the phone company; no new listing. Every time I've gone by her office, it's been locked. I started sticking Post-it notes on her door with messages to call me. Each time I checked, they were gone."

"So do you think she got them?"

"Maybe. I think she's been slipping in and out of her office, but it's like she's trying not to let anyone catch her. The notes I left *were* gone, but knowing my dad, he probably pulled them off her door and burned them—"

"Is that what you think, Chelsea?"

Chelsea whirled around to see her father, tall, square jawed, eyes darkened to the color of coal.

"I'm assuming that's Amber on the phone?"

Chelsea's mouth dried up. She blinked, hard. The receiver turned to lead in her hand.

"I asked you a question. Is that Amber?"

When she finally nodded, he said crisply, "Tell your friend you'll call her later, on your own time. Into my office, please. Now!" With a flick of his wrist, he motioned his daughter to follow him inside.

"I've got to go, Amber," Chelsea whispered.

"Your father, right?" Amber moaned. "Did he hear what you said? Of course he did. Good luck."

Chelsea clicked the receiver into its cradle. As she rose to march behind her father's erect figure, she replayed the conversation in her mind. Her father had caught her on the phone when he'd ordered her not to talk. That alone would make him angry. More than angry. But she'd broken the code of silence and spoken of Diane. That made her offense ten times worse. Bracing herself, Chelsea watched as her father swung open the door to his office.

Suddenly, Chelsea saw herself in a mental snapshot: small, round-shouldered, trying to take up as little space as possible. It was wrong. She was old enough to ask the questions she wanted to ask, and old enough to demand some answers. Diane had taught her that. Squaring her shoulders, she tried to look as cool and deadly as her father. As long as there was going to be a battle, she might as well really face him. Maybe now was the time. For herself.

For Diane.

2

"Correct me if I'm wrong, but I recall having clearly told you not to use the phone for personal calls." John Smythe walked behind his large, granite-topped desk and dropped into a black swivel chair. He pointed at a chair in a way that let Chelsea know she'd better sit down.

Sitting as rigidly as she could, Chelsea tried to keep her eyes locked onto her father's. "Okay. I know I shouldn't have been on the phone, but I was only talking to Amber for two minutes—"

With a dismissive wave of his hand, he cut her off.

"You were on that phone a quarter of an hour."

"No, just—"

"Don't even start. I timed you. Chelsea, I've explained to you how I feel about mentioning Diane. I'm extremely disappointed in what I just heard."

It was amazing the effect her father had on her. She found her eyes drawn to the floor, as if pulled by some unseen force into the steel-colored carpet. The office had been designed exclusively in black and pewter shades, right down to a large oil painting that resembled silver coins pressed into ash. Gray was the perfect color for his office, Chelsea thought. A perfect color for him.

"Look at me, Chelsea. Your being here, a part of Smythe Towers, is important. It's important for both of us. We need to work out a relationship, and I can't do it alone. And I can't have this conversation if you insist on staring at your fingers."

Blinking, Chelsea raised her eyes to meet her father's gaze. His perfectly combed hair and designer clothing, a legacy from Diane, gave him the air of a formidable executive.

"Do you have something to say to me?"

She cleared her throat. "Yes. I—this is hard. I understand that something really intense happened between you and Diane, but . . ." A pressure began to squeeze through her chest.

Her father waited a respectful moment, then said, "Yes?"

"The thing is—" Chelsea took a small breath and pushed on. "Okay. I truly feel that—"

The telephone shrilled. Her father held up his hand, indicating she should wait while he took the phone call. Chelsea watched him waste a brilliant smile into the phone's receiver. It wouldn't matter that the person on the other end couldn't see it. They could feel it. John Smythe could smile through space and air. On everyone but her.

All her life, her father had been a benign but distant presence. Six or seven days every week, he'd vanish into Smythe Towers, like some sort of specter returning to its grave. He'd materialize at a school play, or briefly darken the door to her room to whisper good night. The building had taken over so much of his life that Chelsea had felt as jealous of its steel and glass as she would a real person. It had been Diane who'd changed things, who'd breathed life into her and her

15

father. Diane had been the sinew that connected them both, pulling muscle to bone so that the three of them worked together somehow.

"Thank you for bringing that to my attention," he said pleasantly. "Good-bye."

His gaze once again bore down on her. The air-conditioning chilled the air so that Chelsea's arms seemed to contract right under the skin, but instead of rubbing blood into them she clutched herself in a too-tight grip.

"I apologize for the interruption." His face shifted. Every trace of the smile was completely gone. "Let's get to the point. This is a business, Chelsea. We're here to serve the customer, not chat on the telephone. But more important, I told you in no uncertain terms that you were to forget Diane. I will not tolerate deception, Chelsea. Do you understand what I just said?" He looked at her expectantly. Sullen, she nodded. "Good. Then we will consider the matter of Diane closed. As far as your job performance, we'll chalk it up to a learning experience. Keep your mind focused on your job, and we'll get along just fine. I'll be watching you for improvement."

Chelsea cocked her head to the side and pushed out her chin. Her stepmother had been one of the only people who'd seemed unafraid of her father. Think like Diane, Chelsea commanded herself. Be tough.

Diane. She'd only been in Chelsea's life for a year and a half, but she'd made a big difference in every part of the Smythe home. She moved with supreme confidence, as if she'd always been a part of their lives and the Smythe family had been just waiting for her to happen.

"This room is so sweet I think I'm going to enter sugar shock," she'd said the first time she'd seen Chelsea's bedroom. "Let's change it. Go for something in blue, or maybe mint green. We can rip this old stuff right off the walls, and follow a theme. Maybe"—she'd tapped her chin until her face suddenly cleared— "stripes. That's what I see. Change from sweet to classy." Chelsea had been all set to get angry, but then Diane had turned to her with that bold, clear look she had.

"What's wrong?"

"I like my room," Chelsea had told her. "My real mother decorated it."

Diane had had the good grace to flush. "Well, of

17

course you do. I'm sorry, Chelsea. I'm far too direct, and people remind me of it all the time. Forgive me?"

"Whatever." Chelsea had shrugged.

"I just see you as too mature for pink. No, I see you surrounded by something cool, tasteful. You're so elegant-looking, Chelsea. Truly gorgeous."

"No way," Chelsea had protested. She'd felt awkward, but pleased with Diane's assessment. Her father never commented on how Chelsea looked, only on the way she behaved. And that never seemed to be quite good enough.

"So now I can have a second chance at being a receptionist?" she asked him now. "I don't like the idea of being watched. Why don't you just fire me and send me home? You know I don't want to be here. This job is your idea, not mine."

"So . . . I made you take the job. That lets you off the hook. Right?" His brows shot up.

"I guess. Forced labor isn't always the best."

There was no doubt that she was taking a risk by arguing with him. Lately, he'd seemed determined to rewrite their lives with a brand-new script, one that featured just the two of them finally connecting in the hallowed offices of Smythe Towers. They were now going to be *close*. They were now going to *connect*. On schedule, without any fuss.

"Well, I see you've got it all figured out. If things get a little rough, you can just quit. Bail out. Fold under the smallest criticism." Pointing at her, he kept each word sharp. "I want you to listen closely. That kind of dodging isn't going to work here. You are going to stay, and you're going to learn how to work. I'm still your father. I'll admit, I haven't been the best father, but I still have some authority over you. And whether you believe it or not, everything I've done has been with your best interest in mind."

"*My* best interest? Is that why you won't let me talk about Diane? That's supposed to be for me?"

"What did you say?" He looked surprised.

"Diane. There, I said her name. Diane, Diane. Pretending she doesn't exist makes it easier for you. Not me."

His expression held, but his eyes flashed. "I explained what happened between Diane and me that first night. You know I don't hold with the view that endless talk makes things better. The subject is closed."

19

He'd spoken of it once, and in John Smythe's book, once was enough.

When her father had walked into her bedroom to tell her Diane had gone, he'd kept perfect command of his features. Sitting on the edge of her bed, he'd taken her hand in his. His fingers had knotted tightly over hers.

"I have something painful to tell you," he'd begun. The words had marched over her: Diane was a bad choice as a wife for him and as a mother for her. Now that he'd seen more of Diane's inner nature, he realized he didn't really love her and their coupling had actually been one huge, unfortunate and embarrassing mistake. Diane had been too young for him. He should have seen it. He and Diane had agreed mutually that it was best if she left at once, because the pain was in the lingering. And no, this was not to be discussed. It was his life, and Diane hadn't been, after all, her real mother. Clean breaks were best.

If it hadn't been for the muscle pulsing in the corner of his jaw, Chelsea might have believed that Diane's departure hadn't bothered him in the least. When he'd asked if there were any questions, his eyes made it clear that the correct answer was no.

"I just want to go to sleep now," she'd said.

The next day, he'd decided Chelsea was to work for him, and she'd been following his succinct orders ever since. Sitting in his office now, she realized how alone she'd become, even with her father less than five feet away.

Trying to keep her voice steady, she said, "I'm sorry, but I don't want to close the subject. Have you seen Diane since she left our house?"

"Don't be absurd," he answered evenly. "I haven't been near that woman in almost three weeks. Which isn't nearly long enough."

"Diane had a lunch date with Amber's mom today, and she didn't show. Amber's mom is worried something might have . . . happened . . . to her."

Her father scoffed.

"But what if it did? Who would even know? What if she's hurt or in trouble?"

"That's complete nonsense. I've spoken with Diane."

"When?"

"Last week. She's as alive as you are. Don't worry. People like Diane are indestructible, which in her case is unfortunate." Tipping his chair back slightly, he studied her over the jut of his knuckles. He'd positioned his desk so that the large window was behind him, and in the backlight his face was hard to read. "Of course, you realize what you're doing."

"What?"

"You're trying to deflect a problem by bringing up something that you think will throw me off balance. I won't play the game, Chelsea. We were having a conversation about your job performance. Let's stick to the issue."

"A conversation means two people are involved, Dad. Two, not just one. So if we're really having a conversation, then it's my turn to pick the topic, and I want to talk about Diane!" Even as the words exploded from her mouth, Chelsea wasn't sure who was more surprised. She'd always done her rebelling in small, seething bits that Diane had mopped up before her father had seen. But now there was no more Diane. There was only her father, his eyes squinting into deep lines.

"I have a right to know what happened!" Chelsea forced herself to go on. "Diane lived in our house for a year and a half, and I think—I think that I should be able to—"

Her father's hand snapped up as if to stop any more words from spilling out of her mouth. "That chapter of our lives is over. Let it go. We've got to get on with our lives." Chelsea heard in his voice something warning, ominous, tired. "I feel responsible that I brought her into our existence, and I'm grateful that she's gone. She was exerting far too much influence over you. You've changed, Chelsea. And not for the better."

"But you can't just act like it never happened. *I* can't. I *love* her."

"You'll get over it."

He looked at her so coolly that she wanted to scratch through his veneer until she could find an emotion. "Was it—was there another man?"

"No," he said flatly. "I'd tell you if it was someone else. It would be . . . simpler."

"So we're supposed to just keep on pretending. That's the way you want to handle this divorce?"

"It's my decision."

Trying to keep her features as controlled as her father's, Chelsea said, "I want to talk to her. You don't have to be involved. I want you to tell me where she is."

"Absolutely not!" His dark brows knit together into

a solid line; the muscle in the corner of his jaw began to pulse. "I realize you and I don't know each other very well, Chelsea. That's my fault. I take the blame. But when it comes to your stepmother, you'll have to trust my judgment."

Digging her nails into her palms to relieve the tension, Chelsea saw images of Diane flash through her mind: a wide, full smile, always precisely penciled in; the clear, violet-colored eyes and perfect bone-china features. Expensive clothes that enfolded her, elegant perfume that always had an edge of spice. The gossip, whispered in delicious bits, the polishing of the exterior that Diane taught her. The interior self-reliance. She needed Diane. Her father had his own problem with her stepmother. She could deal with that. But extending the wedge to Chelsea wasn't fair. She tried to keep control, but she blared, "Then I'll find her myself."

Her father stood, slowly. As he leaned forward, his reflection pooled on the desktop. "This isn't you, Chelsea. It's your stepmother talking. I see your face, but I hear *her* voice. It's my duty, no, my *obligation,* to make sure that you don't follow in Diane's footsteps. I don't want you turning out anything like that woman. She left us, and it's over!"

"Diane didn't leave *us*! She left *you*!" Chelsea blinked, hard. Her father flushed, then paled. Judging from his face, she could tell the cut had reached the bone. Drawing himself upright, he walked to the door of his office.

"This conversation is finished!"

"But—"

"Get up. You've just earned yourself a demotion. Starting right now, you're working in the basement of this building, pulling reports."

"What?" It took a moment for the words to register. She'd challenged her father, and he'd crushed her with a power play. The simple decree meant she'd been banished to the worst place in Smythe Towers. Strategies raced through her mind, but none of them except begging would help, and she was in too far for that. Trying to keep her voice emotionless, she stood and said simply, "Fine. I don't really care."

"Then we have an understanding."

"I'll never understand you."

He focused his eyes on her one more time. "When I look at you, Chelsea, I don't like what I see. I don't like what I hear. If this is going to be yours someday"— his arm made a sweeping movement—"then you're going to have to learn responsibility for your own actions. God knows, I'm responsible for mine. Now go home. Report to the basement office at eight o'clock tomorrow morning. I realize you're hurt that Diane has disappeared from your life. Trust me, you don't know how lucky you are."

3

The first thing Chelsea noticed was the noise: a low, rumbling sound, punctuated by a steady, pulsing rhythm. She spun in a slow circle, trying to take it all in. Three sides of the room had been painted a sickly pink, while nearby blocks of equipment hunkered in military gray. Rectangular panels of multicolored wire lined the fourth cinder-block wall; in the center of the room, an enormous computer throbbed as if driven by an electronic heart.

"Welcome to the real working world." John Smythe's secretary, Nola Pierce, grinned. "The rest of us less

27

privileged folk have been working in places like this since the dawn of time. It might be good for you to get a taste of it. Here are the keys. Don't lose them." Stepping over sandbags that ringed the inside of the doorway, she added, "I'm afraid you'll find this more . . . modest . . . than the rest of Smythe Towers." Nola was a plump, fifty-something woman with frosted fingernails and carefully teased hair. Today Nola had dressed with a Western flair, wearing large turquoise earrings that reminded Chelsea of chewed wads of blue bubble gum and a silver bolero tie that had a third, even larger lump right beneath her throat. Diane used to say that Nola didn't project the right image for Smythe Towers, but Chelsea's father wouldn't budge on that point. Nola had worked for him since the beginning and would stay with John Smythe as long as she wanted.

"Cheer up, Chelsea. Smile a little. You're too young to look that mad."

"I'm not mad at you, Nola. I'm mad at my dad. I'm mad that all of my friends are still in bed, and when they get up, they've got the whole day to fill with fun stuff. I'm mad that it's eight o'clock in the morning and I'm down in a basement room, and right outside its door is a parking garage! This place is awful!"

"It could be worse."

Chelsea folded her arms over her chest. "There are sandbags around the door. Sandbags, Nola. It doesn't get much worse than that."

"Now, now," Nola clucked.

"Exactly what are those sandbags for? To keep me from escaping?"

Snorting, Nola said, "Don't be silly. When they clean the floor of the parking garage, the water sometimes puddles and seeps underneath the Communication Room door. We can't let any water get to this electronic equipment, or it's certain disaster. So we put in that ring of sandbags as an extra barrier."

"What about those things hanging from the ceiling?"

"Those?" Nola peered at the star-shaped fixtures that made perfect rows across the ceiling. "Oh, those shoot foam in case there's a fire down here. It takes the oxygen right out of the air so the fire won't spread. If we had a fire in this room—"

"I know, I know," Chelsea broke in. "It would be certain disaster. Let's see, we've got something against flood and fire. But wait? How about pestilence? Got

anything to protect this room from a swarm of lo-
custs?"

"It's not all that bad, dear," Nola said, patting Chelsea's arm. "It's just a place to work. Now then, watch
your step."

Three feet beyond the door, the tile floor raised almost a foot. The furniture, the machines, all were clus-
tered on the elevated part of the floor. Awkwardly,
Chelsea stepped onto the platform. "Why is the floor
raised?"

"Underneath those tiles are all of the wires that run
this show. That's why water getting in here would be
disaster."

"Lovely. My dad's really trying to pay me back by
sticking me down here," Chelsea muttered.

"That's one way to look at it. Or maybe he's trying to
help *me* out. Did you ever think of that?"

"No," Chelsea admitted sheepishly.

"I've always hated trekking back and forth between
the office and the Communication Room, and I've
been telling John that he needs someone down here
full-time. Granted, I almost fainted when he told me
that someone was you. But"—she tugged at her bolero

tie, centering it—"I've been coming down here a long time and I've survived. Perhaps it's not a plan to make you crazy. Perhaps your being here is nothing more than your fair turn. By the way, you look very nice today."

"You like my earrings?" Chelsea asked, squeezing her earlobe between her thumb and forefinger. "They're only a quarter carat, but they're real."

Peering through the bifocal part of her glasses, Nola said, "Very nice. Diamonds. Your dad get those for you?"

"No, Diane."

"Oh."

Nola made it clear she didn't want to say any more about the subject. That seemed to be everyone's reaction. Everyone but Chelsea. She could still remember the first time she'd noticed Diane's diamond earrings. It was the month before Diane and her father had gotten married. Diane had pulled a strand of hair behind her ear, revealing a diamond stud that almost dipped below her small lobe. Even though she was just in slacks, the diamond looked right somehow.

"Are those real diamonds?" Chelsea had breathed.

"Of course." Diane had looked at her and laughed easily. "If you can't afford a carat of the real stuff, then just go for something smaller, but *always* wear the genuine article. I got them myself—" She wrapped her hair around the other ear and cocked her head, showing them off to full effect. "They're each a full carat. It's an extravagance, I know, but my basic philosophy is to go after what I want and get what I want when I want it."

Chelsea had cringed inside, because she'd been taught that saying things like that, right up front, was vulgar. But Diane charged ahead, calm and easy.

"You know, Chelsea, I didn't wait for any man to give these earrings to me. I bought them myself, because I take care of myself. Your father understands that about me." Diane had crossed her arms over her black silk blouse, and her fingernails, trim and polished clear, made a perfect line along her sleeve. "I want you to understand something. Even though your father and I are getting married, I see myself as an independent person. I'm still going to buy my own jewelry, pay my own bills, obtain my own clothes. Which," she laughed, "cost about as much as the diamonds." Her expression changed from lighthearted to intensely serious. "You know, Chelsea, I put myself through law school. I created my own niche in the legal world. I make my own rules, and I'll sink or swim by what *I* do. I think you've got that same potential to make life go *your* way. You're beautiful, and you're smart. It's just a fact. No one can stop either one of us."

"I'll never be able to look like you," Chelsea had murmured.

"Nonsense. You look fine. Of course, the truth is, appearance *does* count. There's no getting around it."

Chelsea had looked down at her crumpled jeans and worn running shoes. A thought crept over her. She didn't look good. Especially next to Diane. At fifteen, she was tall, taller than Diane, but she had no style. She'd gravitated toward jeans and T-shirts, and had pulled her hair into a careless ponytail. No makeup. Even though she and Diane had the same basic coloring, Diane seemed to vibrate with intensity while Chelsea felt as though she faded away.

"If I have one reservation, it's that you're not using all of your potential. I'd be happy to help you, if you'd like me to. You'll go from pretty to fabulously gorgeous. You'll see!" As Diane had spoken, sincerely, with complete directness and confidence, Chelsea had felt balm soothe over the sting that the critique of her clothes had made. And as always, Diane had been right. The day of her wedding, Diane had given Chelsea her own diamond earrings. Small, but perfect.

And now, at the mention of her stepmother, Nola merely grunted. Picking up a clipboard, Nola handed it to Chelsea. "Let's get down to business. You might want to write this information down as I'm talking, dear. It's not complicated, but there's a lot to learn. Now, as you know, this is the Smythe Towers Communication Center."

When Chelsea looked at her blankly, Nola added, "This is where all the phone lines for the entire building are located." She pointed to trunks of heavy black wire that sprouted from the floor like the arms of a giant cable tree. "It will be your job to watch over the operation. You'll pull reports, which means you'll run a printout of all of the calls made in the building on any given day. That's for billing purposes. And you'll do some really basic work on that computer over there." She gestured toward a second desk stacked with pleated paper printouts.

Trapped. Chelsea felt the four small walls squeeze in on her. She would be stuck in this room, away from every living person, until her dad released her. She had no control over her life anymore. She wandered the room as Nola droned on.

". . . take long to master. Any questions so far?"

"What's this?" Chelsea's eyes settled on a yellow handset that sat on top of a printer. It looked like a telephone receiver left out of its cradle.

"That? It's nothing." Nola made a small tisking sound. Bustling over to where Chelsea stood, she plucked the handset and quickly placed it into an over-head Formica cupboard, shutting the cupboard door with a firm snap. "Leave it to you to find the one thing you shouldn't, right off the bat."

Chelsea felt a prick of curiosity. Apparently this awful room had a secret. "Nola, exactly what is that telephone thing?"

"Never you mind. We've got work to do. Let's get back to it. Now then, the reports—"

"Wait a second. If you're supposed to explain this place to me, you have to teach me *all* of it." Chelsea moved until she stood directly in front of Nola. At five feet seven-and-a-half inches, she could easily look down into Nola's gray eyes.

"I'm going to use a little deductive reasoning here, Nola. If that yellow thing is something I'm not supposed to know about, then it must be worth knowing."

Shaking her head, Nola stuttered, "Now listen here, Chelsea—"

"Nola, Nola, Nola." Putting a hand on Nola's shoulder, Chelsea gave her a sly smile. "I can tell by your face that you've got a secret. You know how *curious* I am. Why don't you just tell me?"

"Forget it."

"What do you think my daddy would say if I told him you were using that yellow hickey-thing on company time?"

Nola placed a finger on the tip of Chelsea's chin and pulled gently down. Their gazes locked. "Don't try to manipulate me, Chelsea Smythe. I was outsmarting people before you were even a gleam in your father's eye." Wagging her finger an inch from Chelsea's nose, Nola added, "Promise you won't use it the minute I'm out of this room?"

"Promise!" With a slicing motion, Chelsea crossed her heart and nodded.

"Don't you dare make me regret trusting you," Nola said, opening the cupboard and removing the handset. She held up the yellow receiver. "This is called a goat. It's used to check the phone lines in this building." Nola pointed to the wall with panels filled with strands of brilliantly colored wire and said, "Each one of those lines goes to a phone somewhere in the Smythe Towers. There are over two thousand lines, and we have to check them periodically to make sure they're working properly."

"So? How do you check them?"

"If you'll hang on a minute, I'll show you." From the bottom of the yellow handpiece dangled a four-foot-long strand that split midway into two wires. Each splice ended in a silver alligator clip. Snapping one end onto a plastic nub, Nola said, "This grounds the goat. Now this second clip is placed on a separate wire. I'm trying to find a live one—wait." She pulled it off and snapped onto a second wire. "There!" She cradled the handset in her ear and said, "If I hear voices, then I know the line is working. Lean close, and you can listen to them talking. Hear it?"

Chelsea pressed her head next to the goat. Two men, their voices sounding as clear as any regular telephone conversation, were discussing interest rates. Eyes wide, Chelsea held her breath. She was inside a two-way conversation!

"We can hear them, but they can't hear us. And that's all there is to it." Nola unclipped the lines and looked at Chelsea. "Let's get back to work."

Holding up her hands, Chelsea said, "Just wait a minute! Let me get this straight. You can sit down here and overhear other people's conversations? With that thing—that goat? I want to try it myself. Just one time."

"No!" Nola's eyes flashed. "This isn't a toy."

"Oh, come on," Chelsea begged. "I won't hurt anything. One little tiny time!"

"Chelsea Smythe, it's against the law to use the goat for anything but maintenance. You can't listen in! Unlawful interception of communications is a third-degree felony! Do you want to end up in jail?" When Chelsea shook her head, Nola snapped, "Then leave it alone." With a no-nonsense motion, she whipped the wires around the handset and placed it back in the cupboard.

Underneath her breath, but just loud enough for Nola to hear, Chelsea said, "I'll bet *you've* used it for more than just maintenance."

"I never listen in!"

Puffing air out of her cheek, Chelsea said, "Right. You're probably the one person who knows every scandal in Smythe Towers."

"I know what I know from people *telling* me. Not from eavesdropping."

Hope flashed through Chelsea's mind. "Nola," she began, smiling, saying each word carefully. "Since you do seem to know everything that's going on . . . have you heard anything about . . . Diane?"

"That's none of my business."

"But no one tells me *anything*!" Even though she knew she should control her voice, her words came out sharply. "You knew Diane. I bet you miss her, too."

Snorting, Nola narrowed her eyes. "Hardly. I broke out the champagne the minute she left. The truth is, you're a sweet kid, but you've been under that woman's shadow for too long." Crossing her arms over her ample chest, she nodded slightly. "It was my idea to bring you into the office, you know. Your father listens to me."

"Then I have you to thank for all of this. Instead of having a summer with my friends, I get to hibernate in this charming little cave. Gee, thanks. Help me out anytime."

"Don't get snippy with me, Chelsea. I've watched you grow since you were a puppy. You used to be into horses and Rollerblades. Now look at you. Your hair looks just like Diane's. You wear her perfume. Your clothes cost more than I make in a year. Another idea of Diane's. That woman never could leave people alone. She was always out to remake them in her own image."

"So what? What if I have been improved? Why is everyone always on Diane's case?"

"If you want my opinion, one Diane was more than enough."

Chelsea stiffened, but decided to let the comment slide. Diane had rubbed a lot of people, people who didn't understand her, the wrong way. And there was no point in arguing with Nola. She meant well. With a forced smile, Chelsea clicked her pen as a signal that she was ready to get back to work. "Look, Nola, I think we should just drop the entire subject. But I want to say one thing. You've gotten all of your information about Diane from my father. I lived with them both. Not to be against my dad, but there's more to the story than you, or I, know about. And no matter what, I still love Diane."

Nola opened her mouth to say something, then closed it in a firm line. Finally, she made a little sound with her tongue and her teeth. "It's not my place to interfere with your life. But I'll give you one piece of free advice. Just make sure, when you're placing your bets, that you back the right horse."

Chelsea's eyes dropped to the floor. "I know what I'm doing," she murmured softly.

Nola snorted again. "The entire building is buzzing about what went down between your folks, and none of those versions favors Diane, let me tell you."

"The building is buzzing? What do they say?" Chelsea felt her pulse quicken. Snapping her eyes so that they looked directly into Nola's, she begged, "Does anyone know where Diane is? Can you tell me what happened between my dad and Diane? Was it—"

"I don't know, and far be it from me to repeat gossip. I just do my job. I leave the tongue wagging to the younger folks." Placing a hand underneath Chelsea's elbow, Nola steered her to a stack of pleated pages. "All right, that's enough of this foolishness, Chelsea. We're here to work, not chatter about Diane. I've said more than I should have. Let's get down to business."

The door shut behind Nola, leaving Chelsea finally and completely alone. She looked around at the barren walls and the platform floor. The hum of the cooler droned in concert with the whir of the computer, and the white noise made her feel even emptier. She hated the empty spaces of her life, the open stretches where thoughts could crowd and snap at the edges of her mind. Where had she lost control? Nothing in her life was going the way she wanted it to. Unlike Diane, she didn't make things happen, things happened *to* her. Dropping into a brown swivel chair, she gently twirled from side to side. She looked at the clipboard of instructions she'd written down, at the list of jobs she should attend to. If she were a good employee, she would begin immediately.

With a sure, quick motion, she reached for the telephone and dialed Amber's number. On the fifth ring, Amber answered, sounding groggy.

"Hello?"

"Amber, it's me, Chelsea."

"What time is it?" It seemed as if each of Amber's words was spoken underwater. She gave a little grunt when Chelsea told her it was almost nine and mumbled, "Wait a minute. I have a clock. It's . . . eight forty. That's not almost nine. There are twenty minutes until I'm into the nines."

"I've been up since six."

"Good for you. I was out late last night and I was going to sleep till noon." Stretching, Amber gave a little squeak. "What's up?"

"It's just, I was wondering if you could come over to Smythe Towers."

"You told me I wasn't allowed near the place. I thought your dad said absolutely no friends except for lunch. Not that you can eat friends for lunch." When

Chelsea remained silent, Amber sighed. "That was a little, tiny joke, Chelsea. You could at least be nice and laugh. I mean, you did just wake me up at the crack of dawn."

"You're very funny. Ha."

Groaning, Amber sounded as if she were rolling onto her stomach. "Why are you so cranky? Are you about to start your period?"

Chelsea gave the phone cord a snap. "It's just—I've been reassigned to the armpit of the building. My dad got mad and stuck me down in the bloody basement. Then it occurred to me—I'm my own boss now. No one is here to watch over me. So as my first act of not answering to anyone, I'm inviting you over."

"You're sure it's okay to have friends?"

"If my dad finds you're here, what more can he do to me? He could fire me, but I think that would be too quick and painless. Anyway, I've got a moral question to ask you."

"Wait until you're married," Amber yawned.

"That's not the question. What if someone told you a secret about a device, and that someone made you promise not to use it but it suddenly occurs to you that if you used this thing you might really be able to find out some things."

"Chels, it is absolutely too early for this. Either ask me in English or forget it."

Chelsea bit her lip. "Okay, okay. My dad's secretary showed me this thing that I can use to listen in on phone conversations. I was sitting here, and it hit me. Nola says that the whole building is humming with gossip about Diane and my dad. This could be a way to get information, to find out about what happened! I know I promised Nola I wouldn't use it, but if I use it for good, do you think it would be okay if I bent my promise just a little?"

"I have no idea what you're talking about, but it sounds like I better get over right away. Give me a few minutes to shower and I'll be there." For the first time, Amber sounded awake. "How will I find your new office?"

"Go down the ramp to the bottom parking garage and look for the door that says COMMUNICATION ROOM. That'll be me."

"Don't do anything till I get there."

"We'll see. Hurry."

After she'd hung up, Chelsea walked over to the cupboard and slowly pulled out the goat. The yellow plastic handset might give her enough information to finally discover what had been going on between her father and Diane. It was unscrupulous to use it, but hadn't she been at the mercy of everyone else? Hadn't her father stuck her down in a hole where no human ever came? Didn't he think that he had won?

Something Diane had said swept through her mind. She'd said, "Chelsea, there are two kinds of animals, the sheep and the lions. The sheep are a whole lot fuzzier and cuter, but if you put those two together in a room, only one animal's coming out. What are you going to be?"

She looked at the handset, then over at the wall filled with wires.

From now on, she was going to be a lion.

4

"Which one of these lines looks promising?" Chelsea asked herself as she let the alligator clip click along the wall. What line should she choose? Yellow? Blue? Green? Red? What would she hear? Gossip, business, or dead, empty space? While waiting for Amber, she'd tapped in and heard snippets of both business and personal chatter. It was almost like fishing, where she could drop her line and catch a sliver of someone's life. Although she'd heard nothing about Diane, she realized that using the goat could be as addictive as any Las Vegas game of chance.

Squeezing her eyes shut, Chelsea moved her hand along a panel. When an inner voice squealed, "Now!" she clipped onto the wire directly in front of her and pressed the handset to her ear.

"... you've just got to stop. It's simply not worth it. You've got to quit torturing yourself."

"I know, Brenda! It's just my butt is so big! When I walk it looks like two bulldogs wrestling in a sack."

A burst of laughter exploded from Chelsea's mouth.

"You look fine," the first voice went on.

"Right," a second woman protested. "You can afford to say I look great 'cause you're as skinny as a broomstick. I have never, in all of my life, seen a human being consume as much food as you do. And you stay thin. The only thing on me that's thin is my hair."

"That is so ridiculous!"

"It's true. I'm sure you like hanging around me because next to me you always look good—"

The loud knock on the door startled Chelsea so much the handset slipped from her fingertips and rattled onto the floor; the sound reverberated against the cinder block walls like castanets. Squatting down, she quickly retrieved the canary yellow receiver and set it gingerly on the desk. The knocking became louder, more insistent.

"Hang on," she called over her shoulder. "I'll be right there!" It was probably Amber, but it could be her father or Nola. There was no way she could take the chance. Reluctantly, knowing that she would lose the conversation for good, Chelsea plucked the clips that connected the handset to the wall of wires.

Thud thud thud.

In what she hoped was a friendly and guilt-free voice, Chelsea cried, "Just a second!" She shoved the goat into the cupboard, then took one last look around. Whoever was at the door could never piece together what she'd been doing.

"I *said* I'm coming!" Sprinting for the door, Chelsea yanked it open and looked directly into Amber's startled face.

"Amber—hi."

"Hi yourself. Jeez, Chelsea, what were you doing? It took you long enough to answer."

"Sorry," Chelsea blurted. "I'm glad it was you. I had to move some stuff. I was afraid I was going to get busted. Come on in."

When the door shut behind them, Amber gave Chelsea a light hug. "Well, I'm just glad you're alive. I figured maybe you'd died down here or something. Nice sandbags!"

"They give my office a certain ambiance, don't you think?"

"Definitely. Oh, I brought you some cookies to help celebrate your demotion."

"Is that what took you so long? You were getting cookies?"

"Excuse me!" Amber's eyes widened. "When you called, I was in bed! I realize you can just roll out of the sheets and look perfect, but it takes some of us a little longer. Besides, I didn't just bring you cookies. These are genuine Mrs. Fields macadamia nut cookies." Prying open the tin, Amber waved them under Chelsea's nose. "They're made with real butter. When I throw temptation at someone, it's *temptation*. I'm no amateur!" Freshly showered, her brown hair still clinging to her face in damp fingers, she gave Chelsea a broad smile. Amber's large chocolate-colored eyes had just a hint of gold, but when she smiled, they seemed more tawny than brown. Her features were even: a small straight nose, slightly thin lips, tidy brows, snug-fitting ears, but the whole was less than the individual parts. Pretty, but not beautiful. Compact, but not thin. Diane had called her a near miss.

"Enjoy!" Amber said, thrusting the cookie tin into Chelsea's hands. The scent of Vanilla, Amber's favorite perfume, mixed with the aroma of cookies.

"I can't. They're pure sin. I just think of sticking those cookies directly onto my thighs, because that's where they'll go. Thanks, though."

"Oh. Okay. I'll take them home to my mom. She never worries about the bottom line. So to speak."

"But they smell like heaven." Chelsea breathed in deeply.

With a brisk motion, Amber snapped the lid back onto the tin. "You've certainly become disciplined. You know how much I admire Diane, but I swear she's taken the fun out of cheating." Tossing the cookie tin onto a table, Amber turned to look at Chelsea. "And speaking of cheating, before you explain your secret moral-dilemma thing, which I am *dying* to know about but will wait patiently until you're ready to dish, I have a list of messages from last night. If I don't tell you now, I'll forget." Squinting at the ceiling, she touched the tip of a finger each time she remembered a name. "Okay, Brett asked me to ask you to give him a call. Jimmy wants to know where you've dropped out so he can drop out with you. And Todd asked me to tell you to give *him* a call, too." Focusing her brown eyes on Chelsea, she said, "You know, Chelsea, you can't keep them all. You've got to at least throw back the little ones. Please think of me. I have no size limit."

The mood inside Chelsea lightened. What was it that made any bad situation better if there were two, instead of just one? Smiling, she allowed herself to be carried along on Amber's frothy good cheer. In years past, Chelsea had confided everything to Amber, but then gradually, her life had seemed to shift over to Diane. Diane was . . . older. More experienced, sharper, in control of her own destiny. One confidante was more than enough, and yet, right then it felt good to fall back into the old easiness with Amber. It was like slipping on a worn leather jacket: the bends came in just the right places.

With a pretense of looking at her watch, Chelsea said, "Well, anyway, you might as well get a look at the new place. That should take you all of thirty seconds."

Amber circled once, and then again, as if she were trying to carefully string some encouraging words together and in one more turn of the room, they'd suddenly come. "So! This is the new office. Wow. Your dad put you in charge? It's . . . interesting."

"It's a morgue," Chelsea groaned. "I mean, please! There are no windows, no plants, no anything. The parking garage is right outside my door! You don't have to try to be nice, Amber. I'm in hell."

"How long are you going to be stuck down here?"

Shaking her head, Chelsea let her voice sound as blunt as she felt. "I don't know. I'm not really speaking to my dad right now. We had a . . . disagreement. This is his payback."

"It's not that bad, Chelsea," Amber said, reaching over to give her a sideways hug. "There are workers in Mexico who have it worse."

"I'll try to remember that."

Slowly, letting her fingertips brush along whatever she passed, Amber cased the room. She'd always touched things she looked at. Chelsea had first noticed it when they'd gone shopping and Amber ran every fabric of every piece of clothing between her fingertips. "This feels like heaven!" she'd say, or, "Too much polyester—it'd be like wearing a Baggie."

At last Amber dropped into a wheeled secretary's chair, stuck her tanned legs in front of her, and swiveled from side to side. "So, let's cut to the chase, Chels. I must say, when you decide to drop back into my life, you come with style. You said something about eavesdropping? That *is* how you got me out of bed."

"Okay. Before I show you, can you keep a secret? I mean, you truly have to swear not to say a word. Nola threatened my life if I used this thing. You can't tell anyone."

"What is it?" Amber straightened and leaned forward hungrily. "What!"

"It's called a goat—"

"A goat?" She spun to look behind her. "You keep a goat down here?"

"Not *a* goat. *The* goat." Opening the cupboard, Chelsea pulled out the handset and held it up. "This is it."

Amber slumped in her chair. "That's a telephone. They've been around for a while, Chelsea. Are you starting to name yours?"

"Stop it. I'll show you how to use it, but you have to *promise*."

"*Okay*. I swear. Jeez, do you want it in blood or something?"

Biting the edge of her lip, she looked directly at Amber's eyes. No matter what seeds of doubt Diane had sprinkled in Chelsea's mind, deep down she knew that Amber was someone she could trust. Because Diane *had* told Chelsea not to trust Amber. Ever.

They'd been sitting in a restaurant, next to a window that overlooked the city. Thousands of lights appeared to have been flung along the valley floor, cutting the darkness like chips of ice in a black pond. It was a beautiful view, and Chelsea had felt perfect contentment, satiated with food and Diane's company. She'd been telling Diane about plans she and Amber had made for the summer.

"I realize you've always been close to Amber, but, I want to ask you a question. Don't you think Amber is a little bit . . . young . . . for you?"

"We're the same age, Diane. Sixteen."

"But you seem a much older sixteen to me." Diane had leaned forward on her elbows, as if she were shar-

ing a thought reserved just for Chelsea. "If the only en-
ticement to Amber is her pool, well, I can get you a
card to my country club."

"Why are you so worried about Amber all of a sud-
den?" she asked, drawing her arms across her chest.
"Amber and I have been friends a long time. We get
along. What's wrong with making plans with her?"

"Nothing. Not a thing. I just don't want you to get
so . . . exclusive . . . with that girl. That Amber is a
cheerful sort, but she does possess enough intelligence
to be wildly jealous of you." Diane had been winding a
maraschino cherry through a froth of piña colada. On
the last word, she'd raised the tiny plastic sword and
snipped the cherry between her teeth.

"Amber? No way—she's not jealous of *me*. She's got
the most sunny way of looking at people, at *every-*
thing!" She'd shaken her head, as if the idea would
simply fly from her mind and disappear through the
window. "Jealous? I don't think so."

"Don't be fooled, sweetheart. She's a good connection, because of her father. Keep her as a friend, of
course. But I happen to know she's seeing a doctor in

our building. Now, this is strictly confidential. Can I trust you?"

"Sure."

"The doctor is a friend of mine."

"What's his name?"

"It's unimportant." Diane waved the question away. "Amber is getting shots to lose weight. The reason? I think that's obvious. She's jealous of you."

"No way!" Chelsea protested. "I mean, I believe you about the diet part, but not about the jealousy part."

"Watch the way she stares at you. It bothers her that you're thinner than she is. It drives her insane that you look so much better than she does. Oh, she tries. She wears all the right clothes to cover her flaws. But she can't cover up the way she feels about you. I think every time something bad happens in your life, Amber is secretly glad. She's always looking for that little chink in your armor. Be careful of what you share with that girl."

"You just don't know her, Diane. Amber is smart, and she's *very* nice—"

57

"She's jealous," Diane had said, cutting the sword through the air. "You need to be aware of it. Trust me."

Diane had a way of saying things with such conviction that Chelsea almost always found herself believing whatever she was told. But not this time. She knew Amber, inside and out, and Amber was pure sugar. She'd let her eyes drift back to the scene outside. Diane, after staring a minute or two, had abruptly changed the subject.

And now, as Chelsea perched at the edge of the desk, she knew that not trusting Amber was silly. Diane had been mistaken.

"Pay attention, Amber. With this goat, I can hear any conversation that goes on in the entire building!"

"Are you serious?"

Stroking the handset lovingly, she said, "You wouldn't *believe* some of the stuff I just heard. It's like Oprah, Phil, and Geraldo all wrapped up together. I was thinking that maybe I could catch some office gossip so I could figure out what's been going on with Diane and my dad."

"Bull. You just want to eavesdrop on other people's conversations. This is me you're talking to, Chelsea."

Pursing her lips, Amber gave her a knowing nod. "This is illegal, isn't it?"

"Yes," Chelsea answered slowly. "But I don't think anybody will find out."

"Exactly how illegal?"

"Third-degree felony." Her voice came out a shade too loud as she added, "But only if we get caught, which we won't."

Amber blinked. "Just because you *can* do something, doesn't mean you *should*, Chelsea." Then, smiling broadly, Amber added, "But if it's to help you . . ."

"All right! Roll your chair over there while I grab one for me." She motioned Amber to where the wall was filled with wires and wheeled a second chair beside her. The two of them pushed their chairs so close together that their heads practically touched. With a quick glance behind her, Chelsea picked up the handset and plugged the alligator clip onto a lemon yellow strand. Empty. There was no voice at all, just the quiet buzz of a dead line. She tried a scarlet wire, then a white, then a strand the color of jade.

"Is something supposed to happen?"

"Give me a second. Okay, now listen!"

". . . *actual amount is closer to 3,000.*"

"*At what rate?*"

"*Four and a quarter with a half a point at closing.*"

"Forget this. Let's try another line." Closing her eyes, Chelsea tried again. This time, it was an insurance call, and the conversation was as dry as rice cakes. Plucking the clip off, she tried a third time.

The two of them pressed their heads together with the receiver between them.

"*. . . pick Alex up from day care. Can you stop at the store? I need diapers, baby wipes, and a can of formula.*"

"This doesn't sound too exciting," Chelsea began.

"Shhhhh!" Amber's whisper was frantic. "They'll *hear* you!"

"No they won't. We can hear them, but they can't hear us. They can't even hear a click or anything when I get on the line."

"*Is that everything?*"

"*Yep.*" The voice dropped suddenly low. "*Here comes my boss. Gotta go, hon. Bye.*"

"Okay. Well, let's try another line," Chelsea said,

quickly unhooking the clip. "You want to try?"

"Sure. Watch, I'll catch some guy ordering pizza. Now *that* would be worth listening to." Amber let the alligator clip click along the wall. Opening her eyes, she snapped onto the wire directly in front of her and pressed the handset to her ear.

After a moment, Amber unhooked the clip. "Nothing. Maybe you should do it."

"Nah—you've got to kiss a lot of toads to catch a prince. Keep trying."

"All right. One more time!" In a voice that sounded like a chant, Amber said, "Oh Supreme Power, give me a line with some hot gossip." She attached the alligator clip to the center of the panel.

"I've got one! Squeeze close so you can hear."

As Chelsea leaned in, the goat pressed between them, the sound of two men arguing filled the line.

"*. . . best thing to do!*" a young man whined.

"*You've been two things I hate. Stupid, and sloppy. There can't be any connection back to me.*" This man's gravelly voice seemed older, and more urgent.

"*Look, I panicked. I didn't know what you would*

61

want. I thought if I put it there it might buy us a little time."

The older man inhaled audibly. *"Dover Cave is too accessible,"* he barked. *"Any idiot could wander in and blow us out of the water!"*

"That's not gonna happen."

"You went inside. Someone else could."

"Yeah, well, I left it way in the back. And I covered it with a blanket. No way is anybody gonna find it!"

Chelsea felt her stomach tighten. The voices on the line were so intense, it made her scared just to listen. Amber's eyes widened as she looked at Chelsea. Without saying a word, they both understood. Something important was going down, and they had become a part of it.

"Before you become too sure of yourself," the man growled, *"let me ask you an important question. What if someone saw you doing all of this?"*

"No one was there—"

"So you thought!" he exploded. *"Think a minute— the trees might have shielded a couple of picnickers. It's entirely possible that you might have been seen!"*

"No, I—"

"You don't know! A witness could ruin the whole thing! The police could have been called in by now!"

"I checked around very carefully before I moved it and—"

"We're talking about millions of dollars! Millions!"

Chelsea flicked her eyes at Amber and mouthed, "Wow!"

"We cannot afford a mistake! Not one single mistake!"

"I realize that, sir," the young man cut in. *"I'm trying to protect all of us. And you're in this deeper than I am."*

There was a pause. The older man seemed to be trying to calibrate his tone. Finally, he said, *"I'm sorry. I realize you did the right thing by calling me. This is a very delicate situation, and this complication is not your fault."*

"I was—I was just trying to do my job."

"Yes. Of course. And for that reason, I'm going to double your cut."

"Double!?!"

"Yes, double."

Hesitating, the younger man said, *"That's very nice of you, sir, but don't you think, well, because of what happened, double is kind of obvious?"*

The older man's voice was sharp. *"I strongly suggest that you don't press your luck."*

Even though they couldn't hear her, Chelsea held her breath. Thoughts raced through her mind like a Tilt-A-Whirl, whipping in frantic circles. They were hearing something dangerous. Frightening. Amber seemed just as intense; she closed her eyes as the voices raged on.

"Thank you, sir."

"Now, all you have to do is move it exactly the way we discussed. What's your projection on time?"

"I don't know. I was thinking it would be better to do this in the dark."

"That will also make the removal more difficult. You can't leave so much as a trace behind. You'll need some sort of light."

"I get your point. What if I pick it up at—"

The ring of the phone felt like a jolt of electricity shooting through Chelsea. She looked at the phone on

64

the desk, then ignored it. Squeezing her eyes, she tried to concentrate.

". . . heavy. Can you lift it?"

Another ring split the air.

"I got it in, I can get it out."

"You better pick up the phone," Amber hissed. "What if it's your dad?"

Chelsea swallowed. The machines around her hummed with electronic tension, matching the tautness she felt inside. She didn't want to miss a word, but Amber was right. On the third ring, Chelsea shoved the handset at Amber and bolted to the phone.

"Smythe Communication Room," she said quickly.

"Chelsea? This is Nola. I'm just checking to see if you're having any problems—"

"No. Everything's under control. Thanks for calling, Nola. Bye."

Without waiting for her reply, Chelsea hung up and raced back to Amber, but Amber dropped the handset into her lap.

"It's over. They hung up."

"I can't believe it!" Chelsea snatched the goat,

pressing it to her ear with too much force. She listened, but there was no sound.

"I'm sorry, Chelsea. When they hung up, I unclipped it. I—I wasn't thinking—"

"Why? Now we'll never be able to find that line again! That was stupid!"

Amber seemed to blaze. "I said I was sorry."

"Never mind. Did they say what the thing was?"

"Nope."

"Of course not." Chelsea slapped her hands onto her thighs. "They didn't say, so now we'll never know. That's my life in a nutshell. I get just one tiny piece of information, but never enough to understand the whole picture. It's like with Diane. I know a little bit, but nothing more. I want to know!"

"Listen to what you are saying, Chelsea." Amber's voice was low, calm. "These are strangers. We eavesdropped on strangers. We don't know what they were talking about. They could have been talking about cheese sandwiches. You're getting ballistic over nothing."

"Excuse me, were we listening to the same conversation? Cheese sandwiches that are worth millions of dollars? Right. Cheese! Give me a break!"

Amber narrowed her eyes. "You don't have to get sarcastic, Chelsea. I'm saying we don't know. Chill a little."

But Chelsea felt like a rope stretched thin.

Each stolen word of the earlier conversations had been a brushstroke on a painting, filling in some part of a canvas until a tiny edge of a life emerged. But this one had been different. The picture was of something both thrilling and frightening. The words teased, tantalizing her with possibilities. The men had talked of hiding something. Something worth money. Something worth millions. If she found it, maybe she could grab a piece of fame. Independence. Power. She could let it go, or she could be a lion.

"It's over, Chelsea. There's nothing we can do about it. Besides, I think this eavesdropping thing is a bad idea. Are you okay?"

"I'm fine."

"Why are you getting your purse? What are you doing?"

Pulling Amber to her feet, Chelsea said, "We're leaving."

"Where?"

"Where do you think? We just heard something incredible. I'd say the drive will take"—she looked at her watch—"less than forty minutes."

"You mean you want to go to Dover Cave?" Amber's voice shrilled. "Are you *crazy*?"

"Nope. I'm ready to blow this place and find out what's going on up there. You tapped into that conversation, out of a whole wallful. It's a sign. Let's run with it." She shoved Amber, one step at a time, toward the door.

"But, wait a minute! What about your job? What about your dad? What if we get caught?"

"We won't. Stop arguing! Think of what we just overheard those men saying. What do you think they were talking about? The Boy Scouts? They were doing something illegal, something worth millions. We're going, Amber. Let's do it."

5

The damp smell mingled with the bite of green pine as Chelsea and Amber snaked their way along the road. Dover Lake was a freshwater pond at the top of Mullhollow Canyon. Most hikers and tourists preferred one of the two larger, deeper lakes that marked the twelve-mile canyon road. The first four miles of canyon sprouted chalets or expensive but primitive-looking log-style homes. Zoning laws forbade buildings further up. Dover Lake was the end of the line, a pristine prize for those determined enough to make it to the top. Squinting through her windshield, Chelsea saw granite slabs of rock jutting into the sky, as if they were sentries guarding the sliver of road.

"That's the turnoff, isn't it?" Amber asked. She pointed to a small sign that said SOUTHWEST END, DOVER LAKE.

"That's it! Great, we're getting closer!" Snapping on her blinker, Chelsea turned off onto a smaller, two-lane road, the end of which wrapped the lake like the letter Y. Another four miles and they'd be there.

With her right hand, Chelsea lifted her sunglasses and pinched the damp spot on the bridge of her nose. She tried not to notice the way Amber fidgeted in the seat beside her.

The conversation Chelsea had heard kept running through her mind as she tried to figure out what the snippets of phrases meant. The one that kept reverberating was "millions of dollars." Now that Diane was gone, her father dribbled money to her in tiny little bits. A lesson, he'd told her, in the work ethic, but Chelsea knew it was to give him more control. But what if *she* were able to take control? The seed of fantasy had taken root and flourished. The more she replayed the men's conversation in her mind, the larger the pile of money grew. She'd find the treasure, turn it in to the police, and bask in the resulting fame. Of course, there'd be a reward. There would have to be. And she could take it and declare her independence and—

"What are you thinking about?" Amber asked. "You haven't said two words to me, and you're sitting there grinning."

"Nothing. Just how cool this is going to be. I mean, it's exciting! Most of our friends don't get to do anything more than cruise the malls, and we've tumbled onto a mystery!" She took a quick glance at Amber. "What? You look like you don't believe me."

"I just see some problems."

"Like?"

"Like . . . have you thought about what your dad is going to say when he finds out you've taken off on a workday?"

"He'll believe the message on E-mail telling him I had cramps. He had some meeting somewhere, anyway. Besides, he can't demote me any farther down than the basement." Biting the edge of her lip, she added, "We're solving a mystery. That's the most important thing. That's all I want to think about. You heard the conversation."

"I'm not exactly sure what I heard. We're taking a pretty big risk, and I have no idea what for."

"There's no danger in going for a little hike," Chelsea scoffed. "You've been complaining that we never do stuff together. Well, I've included you on the adventure of a lifetime."

"I still think we should have told someone about this."

Snorting, Chelsea said, "Like who?"

"I know your dad has a temper, but he also owns the building. He might have been a good one to tell. Or maybe the police—"

"Give me a break! Hello! Think a minute, Amber. It's against the law for us to be using the goat. If we ever went to the police, *we're* the ones who'd get arrested! And if I told my dad, he'd *kill* me. My dad is a definite no, the police are out. That's why we've got to go and check it out ourselves! We already decided to do this, and I don't want you backing out on me."

Amber's voice was low. "Why do you keep saying 'we'? Do you realize we've run out of your work, driven halfway up a canyon, and you've never asked me if I wanted to go? You just shoved me out the door like whatever *you* decided is the same as what *we* decided! You didn't used to be like that, Chelsea. Remember the old days? You used to ask."

"Are you saying you don't want to go? Why not?"

Flinging up her hands, Amber said, "Hallelujah! She's actually asking my opinion. Well, I'd turn back because it's stupid and dangerous. Two very good reasons."

"Look, Amber, if we find something illegal, I promise we'll go to the police. I've thought it through. At the very least, we'll get a reward."

Amber clicked her tongue on the roof of her mouth and stared at Chelsea. "Excuse me? You're delusional! You've taken one piece of a conversation and gone and made it into this big . . . thing. You're spending reward money before we've even seen the bloody lake. Think a minute, Chelsea. This could be a drug deal. We might get shot. My idea is that we quit while we're ahead."

"There's money in that cave, I feel it."

"Right. A treasure is just sitting in a cave." Amber

shoved herself back into the seat. "Okay, for one, ridiculous minute, let's say you're right. We go in, and we find a pot of gold. Then what? We can't tell anyone we used the goat. Third-degree felony, remember? How are we going to explain being here?"

"Easy! We could tell the police that we just *happened* to be hiking, and we just *happened* to discover the gold or whatever it is that those guys are hiding. We'd probably end up in the newspaper!"

"On the obituary page!" Amber shot back. "You've got a death wish, Chelsea. I'm sorry, but this is stupid. Really, really stupid."

"Fine. Don't go."

"Maybe I won't." Finger by finger, Amber pressed the cuticles back from her nails.

They fell into silence as the road took another twist. Most of the trees along the narrow road were aspen, which grew in thick patches. Raven shadows inked beneath scrub trees. Chelsea's mood darkened to match them. Now she remembered why she'd drifted from Amber to Diane. Diane rushed ahead, ready to grab on to life. She wasn't afraid. Amber was milk toast; she was fluffy and fun, but when it came to action she would just hang back and analyze. Maybe Chelsea had outgrown her. But now that Diane was gone, Amber was all she had.

Chelsea punched a button, and the driver's side window glided down. Cool air splashed her face; strands of hair whipped around her neck like tiny ropes. Now she could hear the outside. Tops of the quaking aspen seemed to rustle like paper lanterns in the wind, swaying in a gentle, waterlike rhythm. Around another bend the growth thinned to reveal Dover Lake, a steely patch of blue, flecked with tiny whitecaps.

"Aren't you going to say anything?" Chelsea murmured.

"Nope."

"Come on, Amber, let's not argue. In less than ten minutes, we'll know what's inside the cave. Let's both lighten up, okay? Please?"

With her peripheral vision, Chelsea saw Amber staring at her. Amber's head shook slightly, like an old person with palsy. It was unnerving. Finally, Chelsea said, "What's wrong now?"

"Have you noticed that all of these parking spots we've passed have been empty? There hasn't been a single car in any of them. We're all alone."

"Well, just think a minute. That's probably why the man hid the treasure way up here. I'll bet our guy knows how secluded the cave is, so he figured he could stash his stuff completely unnoticed. Quit being so paranoid and have some fun with this."

The wind blew a few strands of hair into the corner of Amber's mouth. She yanked them away impatiently.

Wheels crunched on gravel as Chelsea eased the car into a paved alcove. Like all of the others they had passed, this spot was empty. Trees arched their arms overhead, casting mottled shadows into the interior of the car.

Amber heaved a sigh. "I just hope you know what you're doing."

"I promise I do. Let's go!"

As they got out of the car, Chelsea added, "If it makes you feel better, I've got one of those police flashlights in the trunk of my car, you know, the black metal kind that you can smash someone's skull with? It was a birthday present from my dad." She opened the trunk, grabbed the flashlight, and held it up triumphantly.

A loud caw from a pinyon jay split the stillness. It whacked its wings, then exploded from the foliage nearby.

"What's that?" Amber squealed.

"It's just a bird!" Craning back her neck, Chelsea tried to absorb the jewellike colors of the lake and trees. "This is beautiful!"

"Our dead bodies will look stunning against this lovely natural panorama."

Gritty sand worked into Chelsea's shoes as they began their descent down the dirt trail. It was fifty feet to the shore, and the path wound like a discarded necklace through aspen and evergreen until it emptied into the lake. The morning seemed to be folding in on itself as they made their way down toward the water's edge.

"I wish I'd worn long pants instead of shorts," Amber complained, smacking her palm onto her bare thigh. "The bugs are already dining on me."

"At least you look like you're ready for a hike. I know I should have changed, but I didn't want to take the time. It's already"—she glanced at her watch—

"eleven-thirty." Stumbling on a stone, Chelsea added, "My shoes are going to be completely hashed!"

"We'll just have to go shopping and buy you a new pair," Amber puffed. "Now *that's* what I consider fun."

The closer they got to the water's edge, the more excitement Chelsea felt. The last leg of the trail seemed wilder than the first. Their breathing was punctuated by the buzz of insects and the scraping noise their feet made against the packed earth. Straight ahead, Chelsea saw a large group of boulders covered with patches of green that ranged from lime to dark olive. If she hadn't known the cave opening was beyond the jut of stone, she never would have found it. It couldn't be seen from the path.

"It's over to the right, just behind those rocks," she announced. "I think it's definitely easier to wade around those boulders than climb over them." Kicking off her heels, she hiked up her white linen skirt and yanked off her panty hose. "We can leave our stuff here," she told Amber, dropping her things where she stood.

Amber sank to the sand, pulled off her sandals, and set them next to Chelsea's shoes and crumpled panty hose. Her expression stony, she rolled to her knees, then stood.

With the flashlight cocked under her arm, Chelsea gingerly tested the water. The icy temperature felt like a slap against raw skin.

"How is it?"

"Not too bad!" Chelsea lied. "Come on—but be careful. The water's got some slimy gunk in it. Don't slip!"

As Chelsea turned, she felt Amber take a pinch of the back of her shirt. "If I fall down, I'm taking you with me."

Small, moss-covered stones pressed into the balls of Chelsea's feet, and as she walked, her arms jerked through the air as if she were an acrobat on a high wire. Cautiously, the two of them made their way around the rough stones, and out onto the shore.

In front of them loomed the entrance to the cave. Chelsea crouched and ran her fingers through the damp earth. "Look—it's all chewed up! Someone's been in here. I *knew* I heard something real on that phone!" She tried to sound calm, even though her heart pulsed at the base of her neck. "Let's go!"

Coolly, quietly, Amber said, "I'm not going in."

"What? Why not?" Chelsea looked up at her. The tips of Amber's hair were burnished by the afternoon sun, glowing the color of walnut under clear varnish. Her mouth had pressed into a thin line. Something about the way she was standing, the way her bare feet gripped the ground and her knees brushed together, made Chelsea think of a small child.

"You can't make me do something I don't want to. I've come with you this far. That's enough."

"But—"

"I think you're crazy. Really, I do. All the way down here, I was wondering why I was going where I didn't want to go, doing something I don't want to do. So I've decided to just say no." She dug in her heels and stood rigid.

"Come on, Amber. Please!"

"The thing is, every time I've gone against my inner voice, I've been sorry. And I've got a terrible feeling about this."

Chelsea brushed at the crust of wet sand that clung to her fingertips. Anger seethed behind her eyes.

When had Amber become so difficult? In the past, she'd always done the things that Chelsea had wanted to do, but today she seemed unbelievably obstinate. Amber stood in silence, until Chelsea said, "So you're going to let me down. Just like that?"

Amber gave an exaggerated shrug. "Go in on your own, or stay out here. I'm *not* going in."

Chelsea looked into the black mouth of the cave, then back to Amber. "You're not going to stop me."

"I'm not trying to."

"If you're going to stay out here, will you at least be my lookout?"

"Try to hurry," Amber answered, her voice tight. Chelsea turned again to the cave entrance. She squared her shoulders. She'd have to do it. Alone. She could do it. It didn't matter if Amber let her down. Chelsea was a lion. She was going to go inside and finish what she'd started. With a breezy smile over her shoulder, she said, "I'll still split the reward with you."

"Just be careful," Amber said quietly.

Although the cave opening was wide, it was short, and Chelsea crouched to get inside. Still hunched, she flicked on her flashlight and tried to let her eyes adjust to the dark gray, then inky blackness that stretched in front of her.

She'd known about the cave since she'd been twelve years old. A lot of kids used to tell stories of ghosts that tickled icy fingers through the hair of any visitors, but Chelsea knew that was just talk. Glancing behind her, she saw Amber pacing the front of the cave, her torso cutting the sphere of light that was the outside.

Was it her imagination, or did the damp air seem to caress the calves of her legs? Something was crawling on her shin! Chelsea whipped the beam of light onto her right leg. Water trickled down her skin in glassy trails.

"It's just water—get a grip," she scolded herself. Her eyes widened as she strained to see what was around her. The air seemed to squeeze out of her in shorter and shorter bursts, until she commanded her body to breathe more slowly. In, out. In through her nose, so that the cool air lingered inside her, then out through her dry lips.

Although five feet into the cave the floor was bone

dry, the coolness seeped around her. Twenty feet inside, and then thirty. In the blackness, her flashlight beam made a more intense patch of light. The cave was nearly one hundred feet deep, narrowing at its end in a deep gash of rock.

"Chelsea, can you hear me?"

Cupping her hands, Chelsea shouted, "Is someone coming?"

"No. I just wanted to know—did you find anything?" Amber sounded far away, as if she were calling from underwater.

"Not yet. I'm about halfway in. I'm going deeper!"

"Just hurry!" Amber yelled back.

Chelsea's shoulder hugged the rough cave wall, the stone biting her skin when she leaned too close. Like a firefly, the beam of her flashlight danced in the darkness, revealing graffiti sprayed on stone, and small, uneven pyramids of stone scattered along the floor. A Coke can glared red in the flashlight's beam. Above it, the words Scared to Death and a skull had been sprayed in fluorescent yellow paint. The sandy floor changed to uneven, solid rock. More graffiti, screaming the messages Satan Lives! and Long Live the Beast!

Glancing behind her, Chelsea realized the mouth of the cave was now a distant patch of light. Another twist, and the entrance disappeared like an eye blinking shut.

Twenty-five more feet, and Chelsea's flashlight hit the final V at the cave's end. She'd made it.

At first she thought nothing was there. More glinting stone, three crushed and rusted beer cans. Her beam cut the darkness like a sword. Nothing. She ran the shaft of light on the floor on the left side, trying to make a logical pattern, then to the right. Black, black, black until the beam hit a patch of color—the red-and-black plaid of a stadium blanket draped over a trunk-sized object.

Chelsea's ears began to ring in an eerie, high-pitched whine. Even though she knew what she'd heard on the phone, even though she'd dragged Amber all the way up the canyon, a part of her had never believed she'd find anything. But it was there, the treasure, the mystery that she'd set out to unravel.

Her entire body trembled. She walked to the mound and ran light across the blanket's tasseled edge. With a quick, excited motion, she flung back the blanket and beamed her flashlight down.

A woman lay curled in a fetal position, her blond hair spilled around her face. The pressure of lying on her side had pulled her lip up above the gum line. For a brief, horrifying second, Chelsea stared at an eye. Nothing but the white was showing, gleaming back at her in the ghostly light. There was no breath, no sound, no life. A diamond stud glittered in the flashlight like a tiny star, and then Chelsea knew. For a moment, she couldn't take it in, couldn't understand what she was seeing, but then she knew. The woman was Diane.

And she was dead.

6

Car brakes squealed as Amber drove into a handicapped parking space directly in front of the police station.

"You can't park here," Chelsea said softly. "We'll get towed."

"This is an emergency. Nobody's going to care where I park!"

During the entire ride down the mountain, Chelsea had looked out the side window, her face hidden, while Amber outlined their next move. They would have to go right to the police, that much was obvious, Amber said. It was the only thing they could do. It would be better if the police called Chelsea's father. And then, for the tenth time, she'd asked, "Are you sure you saw a body? Are you positive it was Diane?"

"Yes. I'm sure."

"But you didn't get a good look—did you?"

"Good enough," Chelsea had murmured. It was hard to speak, to put the effort into making the words squeeze from her throat. There were so many thoughts racing through her mind that it was almost impossible to put them into an order. At first she'd been charged with fright, and had grabbed Amber's arm and screamed, "It's Diane! She's dead! We've got to get someone—the police!" They'd run, so fast that their feet seemed to skim the earth. Trees, sky, the path, they all whirled together as they ran, faster. Harder. To Chelsea, the rough stones didn't cause pain. There was no feeling except her heart pumping blood and her lungs sucking oxygen as she'd run, toward the car, away from the cave and away from Diane's face and her lifeless body. The image had cauterized into her brain. In that split second, everything in her life had changed. Diane was dead. She was cold and dead in the back of a cave.

Dead. Dead. Dead. It was too horrible to think about.

"I'll drive," Amber had said, grabbing the keys from Chelsea's shaking hands. "You'll kill us if you try."

Down the canyon they'd sped, away from the body. All the energy had drained from Chelsea as she sat motionless, numbed by the knowledge that Diane had no life. Every gesture had become an effort as she'd sunk deeper and deeper into herself. The last hour felt as if it had been a week; time shattered into too many pieces to be the remains of just one day. And now, in the shadow of the police station, she was faced with telling what she'd seen to strangers.

With a forced smile, Amber said, "Come on, Chels. I'm right behind you. Everything's going to be all right. Just let me do the talking, and we'll be in and out. I promise." As she placed one hand on Chelsea's forearm, her eyes darted across Chelsea's face nervously. "There's just one thing. Are we supposed to tell about the goat? That felony thing's got me spooked. I need to know what you're going to say before we go in there."

It took a minute for Chelsea to realize that she was supposed to answer. "What?"

Even though they were still in the car, Amber

began to whisper. "How are we going to explain this unless we tell—"

"*No!* Don't say anything! I can't handle any more right now. I'm not sure what I heard, I'm not sure about anything! Let's just tell them about Diane and leave." She squeezed her temples between her fingertips. "I can't take any more—I can't!"

"Okay, okay. We've just got to keep that part of our story straight. Calm down, Chelsea. We have to make sure everything we say matches. That's all. Are you okay now?"

Chelsea shuddered. It was all she could do to not turn and scream in Amber's face. She would never, ever, be okay again.

The doors to the police station were rimmed with stainless steel. Amber pushed one open and guided Chelsea into a plain foyer. As they walked, Amber's sandals clumped across the floor. Amber had grabbed her shoes, but Chelsea hadn't bothered. She'd just run, barefoot, all the way up the path.

Any other time, she would have felt stupid walking into a public place without her shoes. But this wasn't any other time. This was now. The worst day of her life.

Amber frowned. "Excuse me."

A squat, ruddy woman stood behind a glass partition that cut the back part of the office from the rest of the foyer. Looking up at them expectantly, she asked, "Yes? May I help you?"

"I—we're here to report finding a body," Amber stammered. "In Dover Cave, you know, the one up Mullhollow Canyon?"

"Yes. I know where that is."

"We—she"—Amber pointed to Chelsea—"found her under a blanket. About a half an hour ago. It's her stepmother, Diane Smythe. We thought we should come here."

The woman stared at Chelsea for a brief moment, letting her eyes wander over her sand-streaked blouse. Instinctively, Chelsea smoothed her skirt with one hand.

"Is that true?" the woman asked.

"Yes." And then she pressed her lips together, hard. She felt as though she needed to hold on to all of her words or they, and she, would fly apart.

"All right, miss, please take a seat over there." The woman motioned to two chairs separated by a vinyl armrest. "I have to call in a unit. It won't take long." She looked at Amber and asked, "Will you please help your friend sit down? She doesn't look too steady. Then I'd like you to come back here. I'll need to get more information from you."

Amber nodded. "When can I take her home?"

"You'll have to let the detectives decide that. Please, just sit her down."

Punching a button, the woman began to speak into the receiver in a strange string of numbers as Amber led Chelsea away. "Yes, we have a code sixty-six in the main office here. Two females report finding a body. Request an immediate unit to respond to the scene. The body is said to be one of the girl's stepmother. A Diane Smythe. The body is said to be located at the back of Dover Cave, which is situated on the southwest edge of Dover Lake, directly up Mullhollow Canyon."

They walked across the room and dropped into orange seats. The vinyl felt cold. It was hard to breathe.

"I'll be right back, okay?" Amber said.

"Okay," Chelsea murmured.

Amber went up to the woman and began to speak in low, hushed tones.

Chelsea could feel her eyes move inside her skull. She looked around the room, at the black-and-white portraits of policemen killed in the line of duty. Even though there was a No Smoking sign directly overhead, she could smell stale cigarette smoke drifting up from the chair. Try not to think, Chelsea told herself. But she couldn't stop her mind. Diane was in front of her, behind her eyelids, skipping through her mind.

"I hate this," Amber said as she dropped in a chair beside Chelsea. After a moment, she began to drag her sandal against the worn linoleum floor. "I'm so sorry, Chels. I should have gone in with you. I'll never forgive myself—"

In a voice so small Chelsea could barely hear herself, she said, "I'm glad you didn't see her. I just want to make sure they find Diane. It would be horrible to just leave her there in a cave."

"I know," Amber said. She reached over and patted Chelsea's thigh. "We're almost done."

They waited. Amber stroked Chelsea's hair as if she were a child, rubbed her shoulder, patted her back, but Chelsea couldn't move. Head bowed, she stared at her feet, at the dirt that left uneven dark patches against her skin. A tapping sound penetrated the edge of her mind. She realized Amber's knee had begun to shake violently; her sandal rattled against the floor.

Almost imperceptibly, Chelsea asked, "How long have we been sitting here?"

"Forty minutes. If someone doesn't come out to talk to us soon, we'll leave. This is ridiculous."

"I need to tell my dad. I should call. . . ."

"No, just wait. Let the police handle it. They'll probably want to send someone in person."

"But it should be me—"

"Hush. It's not the kind of thing you tell someone over the phone."

Squeezing her palms into her temples, Chelsea tried to hold on. Push the emotions back down, to the dark place, until she could get away from the police station and strangers. Try not to think. For herself, for her father, for Diane. Before, when Diane had left, Chelsea had felt the separation was permanent. But nothing was so irreversible as seeing the lifeless form. She could never make things up to Diane. Whatever had happened between them was how it would stay. Forever.

She heard, rather than saw, the detectives enter the foyer. They walked with sure, firm steps that stopped right in front of them. Chelsea looked up. The first one, an older black man with white, close-cropped hair, kept his expression smooth. The other, younger man held a clipboard tucked snugly beneath his arm.

"I'm Detective Fayette," the black man said, "and this is Detective Beech." He gestured to a slender man, who nodded. Detective Beech's features seemed dragged by the force of gravity; his blue eyes dipped at the corners and the edges of his mouth pulled down. Even his dishwater blond hair seemed to droop.

"Are you the two who said they found a body?" Fayette asked.

"She did," Amber answered, pointing to Chelsea. "I stayed outside the cave. I didn't see anything. But it's her stepmother, and she's really upset."

"And your name is?" Beech clicked a pen in his hand as he stood poised, ready to write on a form snapped onto the board.

"Me? I'm Amber Farrington. F-A-R-R-I-N-G-T-O-N."

After he scribbled Amber's name, he looked in Chelsea's direction. "And you're—?"

"That's Chelsea Smythe, S-M-Y-T-H-E. She's the one who found her."

Beech moved even closer to Chelsea and looked directly at her. His jaw moved, and Chelsea caught a whiff of peppermint. He was chewing gum. "You were in a cave? Wasn't it too dark to see anything?"

"No," Amber answered. "Chelsea had a flashlight."

Holding up his hand, Beech said, "Please, let Chelsea answer the questions."

"The—the light from my flashlight beamed right on her face, and I saw some dried blood coming out of her ear. At first I couldn't tell it was Diane, but then I saw her diamond earring and I knew. It was her." Chelsea's voice trailed off. She couldn't believe how hard it still was to speak.

"You're positive this woman was deceased?"

"Yes."

"She couldn't have been just sleeping? Or injured and in need of medical assistance?"

"No. She was dead." It was strange, Chelsea thought, that she could be so sure. She'd never seen a dead body before. She hadn't even touched it. But what she saw in that cave was completely different from the people who had died in the movies and on television. Diane's skin had paled, but more frightening than that was the lack of motion. There was no movement at all, no tiny rise of the chest or flick of the mouth. Nothing. Just cold, dead flesh with one blank eye staring into the darkness. Chelsea shivered.

"Come on, let's get you girls out of here," Beech said, his head dipping with sympathy. "Some rooms right down that hallway are more private. We'll go there. I'm sure this has been quite a shock for you both."

Amber stood and helped Chelsea to her feet. Fayette took the lead, with Amber and Chelsea in the middle and Beech pulling up the rear.

"So. What were you girls doing up the canyon?" Fayette asked, glancing at them over his shoulder as he walked.

"Nothing. Just hiking!" Amber answered a little too loudly.

"It's down this way," Beech said, gesturing to a hallway on the right. "Do you live up in that area?"

Chelsea and Amber both shook their heads no.

"So, you'd just decided on taking a walk and ended up finding a body. That's really a tough break. Were you planning on going to Dover Cave?"

Amber looked at Chelsea, and Chelsea shook her head ever so gently. "No," Amber said. "We weren't planning on it."

"I saw the cave and thought I'd go in. On the spur of the moment," Chelsea added. "Does it matter?"

"Not at all. Okay, Chelsea, why don't you and I go in here?" Fayette motioned to a tired-looking room. With a flick of his finger, he pointed across to another doorway. "Beech, why don't you talk to Amber in the green room."

"You want to split us up? I don't want to be apart from Amber." Chelsea felt her stomach clamp. Never before had she depended so much on her friend. She needed Amber for balance, to keep her mind straight. "Why can't we be together?"

A look passed between the officers. Fayette leaned over to put one hand on Chelsea's shoulder. "No reason," he said calmly. "I want to clear up a few small questions that I have and then we'll hear from the patrol unit and you'll be out of here. It's no big thing. Don't worry, I'll take care of you."

Amber looked at Chelsea, and Chelsea stared back. What could she say? What could either of them do? With a look of resignation, Chelsea followed Detective Fayette's six-foot frame.

The door shut quietly behind them. Fayette, his dark eyes calm, directed Chelsea to a chair set next to a brown Formica table.

"Would you like anything to drink?"

Chelsea blinked and shook her head. She traced a finger along a crack in the tabletop.

"Are you all right? Can I get you anything?"

"No," Chelsea murmured. "I'm not all right. I need to call my dad."

"Let's just wait until we hear back from the officers. We've sent a unit and an ambulance screaming up there, and they'll be calling in any minute with their report. I know it's difficult, but why don't you just try to relax until we know what we're up against." And then, as if on cue, the phone rang.

"Yes," Fayette said in a low rumble. "I see. No, she's

here with me. Of course, we'll notify her father immediately." He stared at her intently, then looked back at
the phone. "Beech is with the other one. Hold on, I'll
ask."

Placing his hand over the receiver, he asked, "How
old are you and your friend?"

"Seventeen. What's happening?"

Ignoring her question, he said, "Seventeen. I have
absolutely no idea, but it's one hell of a good question.
Right. Certainly I'll follow it up. You're sure on your
end? Fine."

He blew air between his teeth, then dropped the
phone back into the cradle with a snap. It took him a
minute to speak, but the entire time he kept his gaze
locked onto hers. Finally, he said, "Well, that's the call
we've been waiting for. They've gone into the cave.
Dover Cave, right?"

"Yes."

"I've got some good news for you. There's no body.
Looks like your mom isn't dead after all."

Chelsea felt the room spin. "What?"

"I said, there's no body. We may not have the best
police unit in the world, but we sure as hell know if

there's a corpse in a cave or not. And that cave was clean all the way through."

"I saw her! I did!" If what she'd seen wasn't real, nothing she knew was for sure.

"I think you've been playing a little game with us, Ms. Chelsea. I really do. I don't know why you've come into our station with this kind of wild tale, but I'll tell you this. There'd been some pretty nasty things going down in that canyon, and I have a hunch that maybe you and your friend just might be part of it."

"No way," Chelsea cried. "We were on a hike. All we did was go on a hike!"

"Now, that's a good place to start. See, I'm a detective. It's my job to notice things. You are pretty nicely dressed, Chelsea. That's an expensive skirt and blouse, from the looks of it. You said you and Amber went on a hike, but you're done up to see the ballet. The officers up at Dover Lake found your panty hose and high-heeled shoes by the rocks. Now, you tell me, Chelsea, how many girls do you know that go hiking in white, high-heeled shoes?"

"It was a spur-of-the-moment thing. We just decided to go."

POISON

"On a hike."

"Yes."

"And on a spur of the moment, you decided to go into that cave. No particular reason."

"That's right," Chelsea answered. But even to herself she sounded unsure.

"Then why on earth did you carry a flashlight? You really want me to believe you had enough foresight to carry a flashlight with you on a hike you didn't plan on taking, just in case you might go into a cave you hadn't aimed on going into? Then you swear you found a body, but the body isn't there. You see, your story simply does not make sense." He paused, then said, "Did you know Dover Cave is used as a place for kids to buy and sell drugs?"

"I don't do drugs."

"Somebody high might think they saw a body."

"I *said* I don't do drugs. And I don't sell them, either."

Fayette held up his hands. "All right, all right. Don't get all hot. It's my job to get to the bottom of things, Chelsea. And when facts don't add up, I want to know why. Maybe you have told me the truth, but not *all* of it. I have a gut instinct about these things, and I think you're hiding something. So until I know what *exactly* is going on"—he leaned back into his chair and narrowed his eyes—"you're staying right here with me. We've got a lot of talking to do, Chelsea. Starting right now."

7

"All right. Let's get back to what you were doing up in Dover Cave. We had a hit-and-run just a couple of miles from your 'disappearing body.' It seems to me that for a quiet little canyon, there's been a lot going on up there today. Do you know anything about that?"

"No."

"A woman in a Jeep Cherokee rear-ended an old beat-up Chevy. She says the Chevy spun off and hit a boulder, but then it took off before she could get out and help. The only thing she remembered was a lady with a bunch of blond hair. You've got blond hair."

"I drive an Infiniti, not a beat-up Chevy. You can check it if you want. It's parked out front."

"All right. I think I just will." Fayette paused, then looked at Chelsea closely. "Look, I'll make you a deal. You come clean, you can go home. Sound fair? Are you listening to me?"

Even though she was answering his questions, Chelsea hadn't been able to keep her mind on Fayette. She could only turn the same four words over in her mind, stacking them in a column and then breaking them into a horizontal string: I must be crazy. I must be crazy. I must be crazy.

She'd seen a body, but then the body wasn't there. Had she encountered it, really? Had her mind conjured up a picture from deep inside and projected it like an image on a movie screen? If she was insane, that meant Diane was still alive, and a part of her was desperately willing to cling to that, to try and convince herself that what she had seen wasn't real, and therefore Diane was fine. But denying that truth meant that her senses had been feeding her lies. Chelsea felt one physical sensation that was completely real: She was nauseous.

"Come on, Chelsea. Why don't you tell me what you've been up to? Maybe you want to get to know me a little better before you talk to me. Is that it?"

Clutching her sides, she whispered, "When can I go home?"

"We're not holding you here. We're having a simple conversation. You've reported a crime, and I'm asking you a couple of questions. But I've got to tell you, it makes me very suspicious that you're trying to hide information from me. It makes you look guilty. Of what, I don't know. But I think you've got a secret."

Picking up a pen, he tapped it against the brown tabletop. The room was completely bare except for the table, four chairs, a dented trash can, a dirty ashtray, and a telephone. The bareness of the room seemed intentional, as if anything remotely comforting had been taken away and all that could fill it were confessions.

"Okay, Chelsea. Let's start over. I bet we could get further if we were friends. How about it?"

"You'd be friends with a drug user?"

"Is this a confession?"

When Chelsea just stared at him, he went on. "Okay, maybe I was wrong about the drug thing. Just looking at you, I can tell that you wouldn't be involved with that crowd. But what about your friend Amber? Is that it? Was she involved in something bad?"

"If this is how you talk to your friends, then I bet you don't have many."

"Well now. How can I get you to believe in my gentler side? I've got three kids, and a grandkid named Collin," Fayette said in an easy tone. "I like Pepsi instead of Coke, and, let's see . . . I'm a Democrat. But don't tell Beech—he's one of those Republicans, and I try to keep politics out of our working relationship. Now that you know a little about me, I think we can be pals. So, let's try this again. Why were you up in Dover Cave?"

Chelsea shrugged her shoulders, determined not to say any more. Fayette was shrewd. He snatched her words from the air and zeroed in on every syllable, making a case, setting her up. As he quizzed her, one thought clicked into Chelsea's mind like a lock snapping in place. Tell him as little as possible, then leave. If she *were* wrong about seeing Diane, then there was no need to confess using the goat, just as she and Amber had agreed.

"You know, this would be a lot simpler if you'd just talk to me."

Chelsea directed her words toward the floor. "I already told you," she said. "I saw my stepmother under a red plaid blanket in Dover Cave. If you don't believe me, then let me go."

"That's not the part I'm after, but if you want to go back to there, then fine." He leaned forward, letting his hands dangle between his knees. "The mind is a funny thing, Chelsea. You might have seen an old, raggedy-looking log, and your mind painted in the rest of the picture with the face of your stepmom. Could that be possible?"

"No. I saw the earring. I saw the blood."

"You had adrenalin in your system, right? You were kind of scared. Could it be conceivable that you were so pumped, you took a quick look and saw something that wasn't real? That would explain a lot."

Chelsea just sat, staring. After a moment, she shook her head.

"It's important to understand what you saw, Chelsea, because we'd have to put manpower into this if we were to investigate a murder. Now, that will cost the taxpayers a lot of money, and without a body it's not smart to take this any further. I want to believe you. But I'm trying to tell you that I need all of the facts."

"It was Diane. She was dead. That's all I know."

He puffed up his cheeks, then blew a stream of air between his teeth. There was a lean tension in his arms and legs that seemed to go soft right in his middle. His white cotton shirt gaped right above his beltline, as if he were a package wrapped in too little paper.

"All right," he sighed. "Then let's try this. One of the easiest ways to settle our mystery would be to call your stepmom, right now. If she answers the phone, then we'll know you were wrong." Fayette smiled, and gestured to the putty-colored phone. "Go right ahead. Call her. There's no charge."

"I don't have the number."

Even if he wasn't, he made a great show of looking surprised. "Your stepmom didn't give you her new number?"

"No."

"That sounds kind of cold to me. Actually, we've got people trying to contact her as we speak. So far, there's no answer at her work or at her home, but we'll keep right on trying. Were you and your stepmom close?"

"Yes."

Fayette paused, waiting for her to fill in the blanks. When she didn't speak, he went on. "But you say she left and she didn't tell you where she was staying? How about your dad? Does he know how to reach her?"

"When Diane moved out, she didn't say where she was going. She just left."

Like a dog catching a scent, Fayette perked up. "Sounds like there was bad blood between Diane and your daddy. What kind of trouble were they having?"

"Nothing much." She looked at him and said, "They parted as friends. Irreconcilable differences, that sort of thing." Another lie, Chelsea thought, but what the hell.

Fayette cracked his long fingers in an arch, and he looked at her in a way that let her know he didn't believe a word she said. Not one, single word. But instead of pressing her any further, he rubbed his hand over his mouth. He glanced at his watch, then over to the door.

"You're not going to talk to me, are you?"

"I have. I've told you everything I want to."

"That's what I thought. Okay, Chelsea, here's what's going to happen next. There's no evidence of a crime. You're not talking to me, but I guess I can't exactly charge you with that now, can I? Without evidence, there's nothing for me to do but release you and file a report that says nothing happened. We'll keep trying to contact this Diane, and if no one hears from her soon, we'll move on to phase two." He reached into a pocket and pulled out a card. "Here's my number."

Chelsea reached out and took it. It was warm.

"If you decide you'd like to talk, call me anytime, day or night—"

A soft knock at the door interrupted his sentence.

"Come in," Fayette barked.

The door creaked open and Beech stuck his head inside.

"Can I see you for a minute?" he asked, looking directly at Fayette.

"Sure thing. I'll be right back, Chelsea. Don't you go away."

Stepping into the hallway, Fayette carefully shut the door behind him. Chelsea could hear the rise and fall of voices, Beech's whisper lacing through Fayette's rumble. The sound rose and fell. Chelsea watched the clock that hung on the olive green wall: 3:39. The red second hand glided around its face, down, then up, sweeping in time with the voices. Her dad would be wondering about where she was. Maybe she should call him, but what would she say? What did she really know? She felt tired. Bone-crushingly tired. Five minutes clicked by, then ten. The door opened again, and this time, Fayette looked grave.

"Your friend Amber just told Detective Beech about some very interesting things, Chelsea. While you've been playing cagey with me, she's been having a kind of Oprahfest over in the next room. Now, why don't you stop wasting my time and tell me about the goat."

Chelsea's eyes pinched shut. Slumping, she groaned, "I don't believe this."

"You see, your friend Amber cracked just like a nut under the great investigative technique of Detective Beech. Seems like you've not only been hiding things, you've been breaking the law."

He lifted up his chair and set it down directly in front of Chelsea. This time, he didn't seem to want to make friends.

111

"Your daddy's outside in the lobby, and he's pretty stirred up. We're going to interview you, him, Amber, and anybody else that might know something about what may or may not be a crime. Now, let's start this, one more time. And what I hear better be the truth. All of it."

8

"Sit down. Over there, on the couch."

Chelsea followed her father's orders and walked across their dimly lit living room. Instead of sinking back into the taupe leather cushions, she perched at the edge, wary, prepared. From the way he'd driven home, careening ahead of her and smoking through stop signs, Chelsea knew her father had worked himself into a rage. No one who hadn't known him would have guessed. At the police station, he'd looked alternately concerned, worried, intent, innocent. But Chelsea knew. He'd even reached over to hug her gingerly, say-

113

ing, "Thank you for all of your concern, Detective Fayette. I'll get her home now. A good night's sleep should fix all of these misunderstandings." He'd kissed the top of her head, hard, and added, "Don't you think, sweetheart?" while never once meeting her eyes.

And now, as she sat waiting for the eruption, she braced with what little reserve she had left.

"Why didn't you call me? Why, Chelsea?"

"I—I don't know."

"You should have. Then none of this would have started. What the hell did you think you were doing? Do you even begin to realize what you've done?"

"What? What have I done? I've reported a crime, that's all."

"A crime? A *crime*?" He began slowly, but each word became a shade louder, more intense, until the last words came crashing in her ears. "There's no evidence of any 'crime.' But in this case, that might not matter. Thanks to you, the wheels are already in motion!" Every movement seemed to barely contain his anger; he spun on a heel, then jerked across the room in broken fits and starts. Their living room had one large arched window, and through the glass Chelsea could see the dusk overtake the sky. She kept her eyes on the heavens, rather than on her father, when she answered him.

"I told the police what I saw. Maybe I shouldn't have. But it's done, and all I want to do is go to lie down in my bed. I can't handle any more of this."

Her father, who was usually so meticulous about his appearance, raked his fingers through his hair so that it stood up in gray clumps. His tie was loosened. His suit jacket had been thrown across the back of a chair, something that he never did. He'd always hung and folded, rearranged and pressed. But tonight, he seemed wild, unkempt, fierce.

"You want to sleep? Great. Fine. Just go!" As he spoke, he went to the wet bar and began to pitch ice into a beveled glass with such furor that three cubes bounced out; scotch, then water. Jabbing his finger into the glass, he mixed it, then took a gulp.

"Why are you so angry?" Chelsea cried. "What about me? What I've been through? Don't you even care?"

"This thing is a lot bigger than just *you*, Chelsea. It's bigger than *me*. If you'd only called. I don't know where we went offtrack, Chelsea, but somewhere I lost you, and you lost me."

"I didn't do anything to hurt you—"

"Well, you did," he cut her off. "More than you know. There are things about Diane that were none of your business. And now, thanks to you, everything she's done might come tumbling out." He drained his drink, then stared at his watch. Tapping its glass face with the tip of his finger, he announced, "I've got to call Diane again. No one's been able to reach her. The police tried repeatedly, but she's not picking up." He looked at her sharply. "You realize that if she doesn't show up soon, the detectives plan on interrogating me."

"No! Why?"

"Procedure! They've already told me that they look at the person closest to the victim. Only, in this case"— he opened his mouth in a pretend smile—"there is no victim. Just the cockeyed story of my daughter, who told the police what she only *thought* she saw. Hour after hour, being grilled by those detectives, like I was some kind of criminal. Did you know the police asked me if you used drugs? I said absolutely not. Was I right?"

"Don't do this, Dad. Just stop it."

"Here's another question for you. What if Diane never shows up? Have you thought of that? What if she's gone to Europe, or Africa, or has decided to disappear into the bloody Caribbean? How the hell am I supposed to *prove* she's alive?"

"She's dead, Daddy. Diane is dead."

More ice, and another glass of scotch.

"Did you hear what I said?" she asked.

Her father whipped on her with a fury he seemed barely able to contain. "So you're standing by that ridiculous story?"

"It's the truth."

"The truth? What would you know about truth?" His eyes narrowed. "Every move you've made has been deceptive. First, I'm told by the police that my daughter was eavesdropping on *private* conversations. Just wait till the customers at Smythe Towers get hold of that one!" As he held his arms out wide, scotch splashed out onto the thick Oriental rug. "Watch what happens then, Chelsea! See how many customers I lose! Do you know what it's like," he bellowed, pointing at her with a finger extended from his glass, "to have the police inform me that my daughter deliberately lied to them, all the while Amber Farrington is in the next room spilling my marital troubles to some low-level detective?"

"Amber didn't—"

"Yes she did! My private troubles were yanked out and exposed. Did you know that she told the police that I was the one who forced Diane to leave?! She said I was transferring all my attention onto you, because throwing Diane out left a hole in my life. Who does she think she is—Sally Jesse Raphael? What a bunch of garbage!"

"I'm sorry, Dad—"

He shook his head sharply. "No. Sorry won't cut it this time." His face reddened. "You know what really galls me? All this, this . . . *drama,* because you didn't want to work!"

Chelsea jumped to her feet, protesting. "Is that what you really think? That's not it—" But her father cut her off.

"Of course it is. You wanted a way to get out of doing actual labor, and by God, you found it. Well, you've got your wish now. You're not coming back. Happy?" His eyes blazed. "Are you happy, Chelsea?"

He gave her a small, sarcastic bow. "You're fired. Give me the keys to the office. I don't want you in there anymore."

Chelsea pulled her purse from the floor and retrieved the keys. Her father stood in front of her and extended his palm. With a deliberate motion, she dropped them into his hand.

"Fine. That's it. So now you're free. Stay home and spy on the neighbors."

Chelsea stepped forward, her back rigid. She had been drained, whipped, exhausted, numb. But now she was angry. Everyone close to her had deserted her or let her down.

"I made a mistake. I'm sorry. But I'm dealing with seeing Diane dead. I don't care if you believe me. All you seem to care about is what this is doing to *you*. Haven't you been listening? Diane is dead! Somebody killed her! And if you don't believe me, then you're as dead to me as she is."

She was down below the level of the earth, in a maze of graves. "Chelsea, I'm over here."

"Diane?" Chelsea strained to see through the tunnels. She stepped over a white coffin, then one made of cherry wood.

"It's not so bad, being dead. Come this way. Come be with me. You and I are a lot alike, Chelsea."

"No," Chelsea moaned.

"Not when we started. You were a diamond in the rough."

"No. No diamonds."

"But I polished you. *I* did it. You belong with me, here. . . ."

Chelsea came awake with a start. Someone was in her room, sitting on her bed. Diane? No. The form was too dark, too big. Her father. She swallowed, her voice hoarse in her throat.

"Daddy?"

"It's me, Chelsea. Did I wake you?"

"What time is it?"

He made a fumble to look at his watch. He squinted, then said, "Three twenty-three." His voice sounded thick.

"What are you doing—"

"Oh, Chelsea, I'm so sorry."

The minute he stepped closer, Chelsea could tell

he'd had too much to drink. Every motion seemed exaggerated, and the smell of alcohol was heavy around him.

"I was walking alone downstairs. Walking, and walking. Back and forth. Do you want to know what I was thinking?"

"Go to bed, Daddy. It's okay now."

"No. No, I have to tell you. You don't deserve any of this. You're the only good thing in my life. You don't know that I feel that way, do you? No. Of course not. I get mad, and then I yell. I've been trying to *make* things go right. But"—he shook his head—"look at the mess I've made. I've hurt you, and . . . I'm . . . sorry."

His shoulders trembled and she realized he was crying. He twisted his face away from her.

"It's okay, Daddy. It's okay." She sat up. Leaning over, she hugged her father close.

"No, it's not. Those are just words. It's not okay. I've made so many mistakes. I've made a mess of . . . everything. I didn't mean to let the years slip by, but they did. I left you to raise yourself. My work—everything stopped for Smythe Towers. I—I left you alone, and I can't get the years back."

"It was fine. I've had a good life."

"No! Mistake after mistake! You were growing into a woman, and I didn't know what to do. I turned the job over to"—he choked—"Diane! I see what she's done to you!"

"Daddy, I'm fine."

"Diane's gone, so Nola said, 'Bring Chelsea to work! Be around your daughter.' You hate me for it. It's too late." This time, a heaving sob broke the stillness.

"No, Daddy. You're wrong. I don't hate you. I love you."

"I wasn't there for you tonight. I'm sorry," he repeated. "I promise, Chelsea. Things will be different."

"It's okay, Daddy. Just go to bed. We'll talk tomorrow."

"Yes. Of course. It's after three o'clock. I woke you up."

"No. I was having a bad dream. I'm glad you came in."

Leaning over, he kissed Chelsea on her cheek. His stubble of beard felt rough against her skin. "Go to sleep. Tomorrow, everything will be better. You'll see. I love you, Chelsea. More than anything."

*   *   *

Her father left in the morning without waking her. It was noon before Chelsea threw her comforter off and crawled out of bed. She felt hot; sun had crept through the blinds, heating the room until sweat collected in the hollows of her elbows and knees.

Chelsea drifted over to her window and flicked open her blinds. Outside, a flock of birds cut a white ribbon through the sky, piercing clouds like a fluttering arrow. She watched them as they turned in perfect formation, their undersides transforming into silver, then vanishing in the distance.

Her father. Had that been a dream? He'd never apologized for anything. Ever. Was he just drunk? Or had something changed inside him? Could she trust his words? She ran her hand along the window ledge. The curtains, china blue with a delicate pinstripe, had been chosen for her by Diane. Before Diane, her room had been completely different, trimmed in rosebuds and lace by her real mother.

Now she'd lost two mothers. Was her first mother, her real mother, sitting in the sky somewhere, watching what was happening in her life? Memories of her mother were like photos left underwater; they blurred out of focus, fading and warping until there was nothing left. She'd died when Chelsea was only three, and her father had packed up all reminders years later when Diane came: the watercolors that her mother had painted, the photographs of her father and mother together, the silk wedding flowers—all pressed between pristine layers of tissue in the attic. Though he'd never said it, there was an unspoken rule: Don't talk about what's past. Keep fastened to the future, to what you can change. Try to forget the rest.

Once, when Chelsea was ten, she'd seen an old black-and-white movie of *Les Misérables* on the late-night movie station. The mother, Fantine, died trying to save her child, so she'd gone into her father's study to ask him about her own mother. He'd looked up from his writing while she explained the movie and what she'd been thinking.

"No, it's not bad that you don't miss your mother," he'd told her. "You were so small when she died. Just barely three. You can't miss what you never knew."

"But what was she like?" she'd pressed. It was rare to find her father in a mood like this, misty, open, ready to dip back into the past. Even at ten, she'd realized how unique this moment was. She'd felt an urgency to pull stories from him.

"Let's see, what was she like?" He'd taken off his reading glasses and set them on the edge of his desk, then pulled her into his lap. "Well, Suzonne loved flowers. She did your room in pink roses the month after you were born because she always wanted a little girl to surround in pink. Pink was her favorite color. See this?" With one hand, he picked up a silver cigarette lighter etched with roses. "Your mother didn't smoke, but she loved roses so much that when she saw this, she bought it. She thought it was a beautiful way to light candles. She absolutely loved to cook." He gave a sorrowful little laugh and shook his head. "I gained a lot of weight while we were married, I'll tell you. She loved animals. Loved to read, too. Dickens was her favorite author. Always made her cry."

"Did my mom hurt when she died?"

Her father seemed surprised by the question. "No, Chelsea. Her car was going close to fifty miles an hour. The doctor said she died instantly. Don't ever worry about that."

"Are you going to get married again?"

"Well," he'd said, "this is a night of questions for you, isn't it?" He'd squeezed her close, and Chelsea could smell the faint spice of his aftershave. "No, it's just you and me now. I don't need any other woman in my life. All I need is you. You and my work."

He'd meant it. He'd dated only a few women, mostly when he went to the opera or the symphony. But then, he'd met Diane. She had been different from the others—more beautiful, sharper, a woman who could choose instead of settle. Weeks after he'd met Diane, her father had begun to act in strange ways: He'd brought home an Armani suit. He'd started to lift weights. When he bought an exercise cycle and installed mirrors along the basement wall, Chelsea knew he was in love.

"I know she's young, but she's a very exciting woman," he'd told her. "Are you embarrassed by the difference in our ages? At thirty, she's closer to your age than mine."

"Nah," Chelsea had teased. "It's not a problem, Dad. Just don't take her across state lines."

He'd laughed, blushing around the edges of his hair. It was amazing to see her father blush. She'd never seen it before, or since.

The day she'd first met Diane, she'd been prepared to keep her distance, but Diane had focused on her in a way that made her feel special.

"You're unusually intelligent for a fifteen-year-old. And so beautiful! I think we're going to be very good friends. Sit down and tell me about you." She'd sat, cross-legged, her chin resting in her cupped hand, her eyes focused totally on Chelsea. And Chelsea had talked, and Diane's attention never wavered for a moment. No wonder my dad loves her, she'd thought. It was as if whatever Diane believed must be true. Her opinions, her take on the world, seemed to be right coming from her lips. And this reed-thin woman with the china skin thought she, Chelsea, was beautiful. And smart. Full of potential. Maybe, just maybe, things in her own life were possible.

Diane had reached over and taken her hand. "Listen to me," she'd sighed. "I'm going to take a bit of getting used to. I'll make mistakes." She'd put her arm around Chelsea, lightly, effortlessly. "I'll never be your mother, Chelsea. I don't know how. You know, I've never had a family, so this relationship stuff is going to be new to me, too. But it'll be wonderful, you'll see."

And as with every decree Diane ever made, she was right. Until it ended in the back of a cave.

The cave. The body. Her father. Too many thoughts. Chelsea pressed her hands into her eyes. She should try to stop thinking. What good did it do to remember, to ask endless questions? Take a hot shower, Chelsea told herself. Steaming water that could wash away all she'd seen, and maybe wash away her thoughts as well.

Suddenly, doorbell chimes split the air. Who? Chelsea asked herself. She flattened her head against her window so she could see a few feet of their driveway. A blue Audi. Amber.

9

"Chelsea! Hi. Is your dad here?"

"No."

"Good. I can only deal with one angry Smythe at a time." Amber stood in the doorway, clutching a bouquet of yellow baby roses, and the sweet smell enveloped Chelsea as Amber reached over to give her a tiny hug. "I know I'm not a person you want to see, but I need to talk to you. Can I come in?" Amber began to do what she always did when she was nervous—chatter. She talked in an unstoppable stream, as if Chelsea would be swayed by the flow of her words. "You look

129

awful, Chels. Have you even slept? No, I bet you didn't close your eyes even once last night. Well, believe it or not, I fell right to sleep. Being scared and upset really drained me, so when my head hit the pillow, I was *out*." She turned the roses between her hands, and buds of baby's breath dropped like flakes of snow. "You're mad because I told the police about the goat, right? I know, I know, we agreed, but they *grilled* me. So I'm here to ask you to forgive me. So can I come in?" Without waiting for a reply, Amber stepped past her. The doorknob remained in Chelsea's hand. Once she realized Amber was going to stay inside, Chelsea shut the door with a bang.

"Anyway, here's a flat-out bribe," Amber said, smiling sheepishly. "I know you like yellow roses, which, by the way, stands for friendship. They're to say, 'I'm sorry I have such a big mouth.'"

"It's not just the goat, Amber. It's the things you told about my dad and Diane. My dad's worried that he could get in trouble because of what you said."

Amber's mouth widened. "Me!?! I didn't say anything, except that Diane packed up a few weeks ago. What's so secret about that?"

"All I know is that my dad told me that you were spilling their marital troubles. He was really . . . annoyed."

Lifting her chin a notch, Amber eyed her defensively and when she spoke, her voice had a challenge in it. All traces of the cheery acquiescence disappeared. "Look, maybe I did say too much. It's just, there was so much *pressure*. Detective Beech said we couldn't be the ones to decide what information was important and what wasn't, and things just kept coming out of my mouth. I was truly trying to help."

"I wouldn't exactly call what you did help."

"Right. Well, you're right. I screwed up. I tried to talk to you at the station, but they wouldn't let me near you, and then your dad came, and then my mom showed up and took me home."

Chelsea's head throbbed. There was too much to think about. Too many thoughts pounding behind her eyes. "The problem is, they think my dad might be involved somehow."

"What? No way. I don't believe it."

"Believe it."

Placing her fingers over her lips, Amber thought a

moment, her gaze zigzagging the room until settling on Chelsea.

"Look, I know I shouldn't have said anything about your dad and Diane. It never once occurred to me that they'd think . . . I really am sorry."

"It's okay. Forget it."

"The thing is, right now we've got to stick together, Chels. *We* is all *we* got." Amber rooted herself in front of Chelsea and thrust the roses toward her middle. "Are you listening to me?"

"Yes. I'm just . . . tired." Slowly, carefully, Chelsea lifted the flowers from Amber's outstretched hand. "Don't worry about what you said. It doesn't matter. No one believes what I saw, anyway. Diane's probably fine. I'm probably crazy." She drank the scent deeply, murmuring, "Maybe that's the short answer; I'm insane."

"There's nothing wrong with your mind. I believe you. I believe Diane is dead. Chelsea Smythe, sometimes you're a pain, but you're the sanest person I know."

The words caught Chelsea by surprise; they sank through her skin like water on parched earth. Images had whirled relentlessly through her mind as she tried to patch present to past, and now she had a refuge. Amber believed her. Amber believed in her.

"Here's what we're going to do. We're going to get you dressed." When Chelsea started to protest, Amber cut in with, "Don't worry, I'll wait while you take a shower. We're going to go over what you saw. I thought about it all morning, and I've been able to come up with two things. Number one: Whoever killed Diane moved her body. That's why it wasn't there when the police showed up. And number two"—she held up her index and middle fingers like a Girl Scout taking an oath—"Diane's murderer is still in Smythe Towers. We heard him talk about it, and the call came from somewhere in that building. You know what? This guy's thinking he's home free. Fine. Let him. If the police won't find him, then we will."

Amber drifted over to Chelsea's closet and pulled open its large French doors while Chelsea towel-dried her hair at her vanity. The top of the closet was crammed with plush animals of every shape and size: Dogs, rabbits, long-haired kittens, and monkeys had been stacked like blocks along the shelf in a strange cacophony of multicolored fur.

"I don't know how you can sleep with all of these glass eyes staring at you," Amber said as she let her finger drift along the row of stuffed animal feet.

"I can't. That's why I keep the closet doors shut. They used to be on my bed, but Diane"—Chelsea swallowed, then went on—"Diane put them away."

"Well, I think they look sad. I'll close your closet so I don't have to see them."

"You do that. But I'm almost positive my stuffies don't hold a grudge. You are such a bleeding heart."

Amber crossed the room and leapfrogged onto the bed. Pulling her legs up, Indian-style, she said, "Are you ready to work?"

"I don't know what good this'll do. I've already told everything to the police."

"And they blew you off, right?" Amber nodded knowingly. "Forget them. I think we need to do it for us. And for Diane." Amber rummaged through Chelsea's nightstand drawer and pulled out a small notebook and a green pen. Clicking one end with her thumb, she looked over at Chelsea and said, "I know this is going to be hard. I want you to try to pull away from how bad it hurts, and just try to concentrate on the facts. Okay? Do you think you can do it?"

Without speaking, Chelsea nodded. She took a few deep breaths. She knew she'd have to think analytically, as if she were putting together pieces of a puzzle instead of remembering someone she loved lying against a cave wall.

"Are you okay? You look kind of pale."

"I'm fine. I'm ready."

"Let's start at the very beginning. Do you think you could go back to the Smythe Communication Room and find the wire we heard the call on? I was thinking that maybe we could trace the line backward to the source. It's one way we could find who the man is."

"I—I don't know."

"Try and think."

Chelsea squeezed her eyes shut and imagined the wall with all of its colored lines and plastic nubs. Shaking her head, she said, "I couldn't find it again. I'm sorry."

Sighing, Amber murmured, "Don't worry about it.

Me neither. I can't even find my car after I've parked. I was just hoping your memory for that kind of stuff was better than mine."

"I could probably get in the general area," Chelsea said slowly. "But we'd have to listen in on hundreds of wires to find the right one. And then it would only work if the man was on the line at that exact moment we tapped in. And even *then*, I'm not sure I'd recognize his voice. It's really a long shot, Amber."

"You want to know something weird?" Sinking back into Chelsea's bed, she pulled a pale blue pillow onto her stomach. "The older guy's voice sounded familiar to me. I can't exactly put my finger on it. . . . Did he sound familiar to you?"

"No." Chelsea twisted in her seat so she could read Amber's face, but all she could see over the pillow were Amber's chin and the sharp rise of her nose. "Are you sure? This could be important."

"No, no, no. It's more of a . . . feeling. I don't know. It's probably nothing. But maybe if I heard him one more time, it'd click. I'd sure like to find that wire again. Do you think Diane knew her killer?"

"I don't know." The question made Chelsea sick.

She pictured Diane at her desk, talking on her phone, scribbling on a yellow notepad as she spoke to a client. What if—suddenly, a thought burst through her mind.

Amber leaned forward. "What? You just had an idea. Your eyes look like they're going to pop."

"There might be a way to catch him." Chelsea put a space between each word. "The killer is in Smythe Towers. Every call in that building is recorded. We could type Diane's phone number into the computer and get a printout of the calls she made. Then we could dial and see if we recognized the man's voice."

"This could work! Chelsea, you're brilliant!"

"Except—" Chelsea dropped her head in her hands. Pinching her forehead between her fingers, she moaned, "We've got a problem. We can't get into the Communication Room."

"Why not?"

"I've been fired. My dad took the keys."

Amber pulled her chin to her chest and stared at Chelsea, her eyes wide. "That's a big problem. We need to get in there. Is there any way you could get him to change his mind and get the keys back?"

"I don't know. Give me a second to think." Pouring

some leave-on conditioner into her hands, Chelsea rubbed it through her hair to the very tips. Wet, the strands deepened to the color of caramel. Wrapping a lock around her finger, she thought of her father, sitting on her bed in the middle of the night, promising to make things better. The picture was of him crying, his veneer cracked wide enough for her to see the chaos inside. It had never occurred to her that what she had done might have hurt him. She never once thought that her father might be wrestling with his own demons. She didn't need to stir those waters yet.

"Are you okay, Chelsea?"

"My dad and I—we started to talk. I don't want to push it right now. If I ask for the keys now he's going to want to know why and—wait a second!"

"Now what? Chelsea, you look like you're going to stroke out. What?"

"I just thought of something. My dad's got a key ring in the top drawer of his desk. The desk in his study. The key to the Communication Room's on it and—I think one of them is to Diane's office."

Amber threw the pillow to the side and sat up. "We'll get copies made. Today. There's a little hole-in-the-wall store that makes keys while you wait. Chelsea, I know it's sneaky to take those keys, but you and I are the only ones who even believe Diane is dead. We're the only ones who can find out who killed her."

"We'll do what we have to," Chelsea answered.

"All right! Now we're moving." Amber picked up the pen and paper and tucked a lock of hair behind her ear. "I know this is really hard but . . . we need to talk about Diane. Was there anyone who didn't like her?"

"I don't know. Nola. You know Nola—she told me she broke out the champagne the minute Diane disappeared. I think Nola's always had a tiny crush on my dad, but . . ."

Amber twisted the pen between her thumb and forefinger. A darkness seemed to settle over her features. "Wasn't Nola the one who used to work in the Communication Room? Could it be possible that she used the goat to eavesdrop on Diane? If she hated her enough, Nola might have tried to blackmail Diane into leaving."

Snorting, Chelsea said, "Right. When you meet Nola, you'll know how ridiculous you sound. There is no way it's Nola. Trust me."

"Did Diane have a secretary? Could we talk to her?"

"Nope. When she moved into the building, she got one of the little offices. A nice desk and a couple of file cabinets. That was it."

"So, no secretary. How about people she took to lunch? Talked with on the phone. People we could ask about her. You know, friends?"

"Let me think a minute. Friends." Chelsea gave a bare laugh. "I don't know. Now that I think about it, I don't remember Diane being close with anyone but me or my dad. She *impressed* everyone, but I guess personally Diane just seemed to rub people the wrong way. The list of people I know who really liked her is short. Me, and maybe you." She watched Amber's eyes fade down. "At least, I'm assuming you liked her. You always said how pretty Diane was, and how smart you thought she must be."

"Right." Amber rolled back and landed spread-eagle on Chelsea's bed. Staring at the ceiling, she made an arch with her fingers, then let her hands flop back onto the bed.

"What's wrong?"

After a pause, Amber said, "I think—I think you'd

have to put me on the longer list. I know that's a horrible thing to say, Chelsea. There I go with my mouth again. I should just learn to shut up, but, even if you get mad, I think you should know what I really feel." When she looked into Chelsea's eyes, she added, "Or maybe, I should just shut up."

"No. I want to hear this. I thought you said she was a fantastic person."

"But I never said I *liked* her. Her personality. You never asked."

"Okay. I'm asking now."

"You really want to know?"

Crossing her arms over her chest, Chelsea said, "Sure."

"I think Diane was a taker. I think she could have screwed anybody and not lost a second of sleep over it."

Chelsea could feel her heart beat. First her father, then Nola, and now Amber. The closeness she'd been feeling toward Amber withered, and in its place rose hostility. What Amber didn't understand was that somewhere along the line, Chelsea and Diane had merged. Any attack on Diane cut as deeply as if it were on Chelsea herself. Trying to keep her voice even, she

141

said, "It's pretty easy to turn on somebody once they're dead. Diane can't defend herself."

"All I'm saying is that Diane could make people mad enough to kill. If we're serious about trying to find the murderer, then we've got to look at Diane the way she really was. Otherwise, we won't be able to solve anything."

Staring hard, Chelsea said, "You know, this is really funny. I'm sitting here, listening to you try to shred Diane into confetti, and I'm thinking about what Diane said about you. Diane told me not to trust you, and now you're telling me I shouldn't trust Diane. You told the police some damning things about my father. God knows what you said about me. I think maybe Diane was right." A beat later, Chelsea added, "Why don't you leave, Amber. Now."

But Amber didn't move. Instead, she talked to the ceiling, almost as though Chelsea were not even there. "Remember how close you and I used to be, before Diane? I could have told you anything back then. I saw what happened. Diane tried to get you to hate me. You probably thought I didn't know, but I did. I'm not stupid. When we were in the car, driving up the canyon, I was thinking that you'd changed too much. You dropped me as a friend at your convenience, and then you picked me back up when it suited you. That's not fair, Chelsea. It's like you make all the rules now and everybody has to play your way—"

"If I've changed, it's because I've grown up and you haven't," Chelsea shot back. "You're jealous. Diane told me you were jealous, and she was right. Now you're trying to poison my feeling for her and I won't let you."

With a jerking motion, Amber sat up. Her eyes thinned to dark slits. "Jealous? Is that what she said? That *I* was jealous? You don't get this at all, do you? It wasn't *me* that was jealous, it was Diane. She was jealous of anyone that had your attention, even for a day."

Anger flashed through Chelsea like an emotional electrical storm. "That is so much garbage! Shut up! Just shut up!" She began to shake. Cold drops of water ran off the tips of her hair, dripping down her back in chilly beads, but it was the emotions inside that shook her until her body felt it would explode. Everything she'd thought she'd known seemed to be turned upside down. But Amber kept talking. Why couldn't Chelsea get her to stop talking?

"I called you in the first place because I missed you," Amber said. "But I missed the *old* you. Diane transformed you. You just didn't realize what happened because she changed you slowly. Have you ever heard the story about the toad being put in a pot of hot water? He'll jump right out and hop away. But if you put him into warm water, and then slowly turn up the heat, he'll just cook. He'll never even know what's happening to him."

"So now I'm a toad? I'm a stupid, boiled toad. Diane was my friend, not my master! I make my own choices. I'm exactly the way I want to be. She didn't control me! No one controls me!"

"Oh yes she did. Princess Di, queen of manipulation."

Chelsea leaped to her feet. "Just get off my bed and get out of my house! If you hated her so much, then maybe you killed her. You were late getting to the Communication Room. Where were you, Amber? Where were you yesterday morning?"

Slowly, with a hard motion, Amber got to her feet. "If you are so screwed up that you think for one second that I killed Diane, then you are truly pitiful. I mean that. You can choose to ignore the whole rest of the world and go on thinking Diane was a saint. The Chelsea I used to know is as dead as Diane."

No! Chelsea thought. Diane had been the one to listen to her, to shape her, to focus on her. "You're the best, Chelsea. You're a lot like me," she would say. "Look in the mirror and understand that there are no limits on your future. Only the ones you put on yourself." And how often had Diane said, "Go ahead, buy the best. You *are* the best, Chelsea, so you deserve it!"

But against her bidding, impressions began to come together, a little at first, then more and more, like metal shavings drawn to a magnet. Diane, laughing about power. "Take it, Chelsea. Take the power. Make the world come to you on *your* terms." Diane, planting seeds of distrust in everyone around her.

Chelsea tried to pull all of the facts into one picture, but everything she'd known about Diane seemed to fragment. What if Amber were right? Had Chelsea been seduced? Had she changed? Was she shoving away her last real friend?

A hand hovered at the edge of her shoulder, like a bird afraid to light. Amber. Amber looked as ashen and shaken as Chelsea felt. "I'm going to leave now," Amber said tightly. "I shouldn't have told you all this, especially right now. It wasn't fair. I'm sorry. It's just, I've been thinking it for such a long time." Her voice cracked. "I'll see you later—"

"Maybe you're right," Chelsea said, raising her hand to touch Amber's fingers. The anger was cooling; the hurt had gone; only emptiness remained. "I don't know what to think anymore. My life—I just—I can't make any sense of it. I know you didn't hurt Diane. I didn't mean it." Tears dropped quietly down her cheeks and onto her shirt. Wiping them away with the palms of her hands, she moaned, "Look at me! *Now*, I cry. I made it through yesterday and last night, but now, I cry. God, I'm so ridiculous!"

"You're not, either." Amber reached into her pocket and pulled out a tissue. "Here."

"Thanks." Chelsea pressed the tissue beneath her eyes, then rubbed her nose. Sniffing deeply, she said, "It's just—this is so hard. Everyone else saw her differently, and it's like, I didn't see anything but the good. I mean, she could be bitchy, I know that. But she made me think I was the most important person in her life.

I mean, she talked to me, you know? She took time for me. It's like I knew somebody totally different from everyone else."

Soothingly, Amber said, "Diane had a lot of sharp edges that you didn't notice, Chelsea. But the thing to remember is that no one else saw her good qualities the way you did, either. Look, I think Diane loved you more than anybody. And if she played by her own rules, in a way, so what?" Amber searched her eyes.

"What do you mean, 'so what'?" Chelsea crumpled the Kleenex in a tight ball. "You just got through telling me she was horrible. I can't keep up with you."

"I'm saying that part doesn't matter. This isn't about nice people getting justice, and people on the edge getting what they deserve. Diane didn't deserve this."

"She didn't," Chelsea said. Choking on the words, she said, "I loved her."

"I know. I really believe we might be able to find who did this to her. If we think. If we don't turn on each other, we could find the killer. Because no matter what, Diane didn't deserve to die."

10

The Smythe Towers parking garage had always reminded Chelsea of a tomb. The steep driveway immediately dipped below the surface of the building, leading to what seemed like a netherworld of dim lights and thick, fume-filled air. As Chelsea pulled the parking stub from the machine and watched the red-and-white metal arm glide up, then down behind her, she realized how far away the city seemed. The sun might be blazing outside, but inside, stripes of neon created the light.

"I think you're smart not to use your parking card,"

Amber told her. "Let's not leave any kind of a trail that we've been here. On our way out, we'll just pay our money and leave."

"I'm going to try to park far away from the Communication Room door, just to be sure no one sees my car." She gave Amber a sideways glance and asked, "Are you okay?"

"Kind of. I'll feel a lot better when we're driving back out."

Chelsea approached the end, took another twist down a narrow ramp, and entered the level where the Smythe Communication Room was located. Finally, she spied an open space in a row of cars that reminded her of teeth with a gap. She slipped into the spot and cut her engine.

"It's possible that Nola might show up in the Communication Room, or maybe my dad'll go down there himself. Going inside is going to be risky. The thing is, he—I don't want to ruin the start my dad and I have made. We both need to trust each other again. And," she said heavily, "it won't help things if he finds out I sneaked into his study and lifted his spare key ring."

"I know." Amber's eyes were locked straight ahead.

"But there isn't any other way. We've got the copies of the keys, and if your dad doesn't find out, then there's no harm done, right?"

Chelsea followed Amber's line of sight to the far wall. Three heavy metal doors reflected smears of light in their shiny black paint. One set of double doors led to elevators, one door opened to the stairwell, and the third to the Communication Center.

"It's spooky down here," Amber said softly. "Especially when you consider that a killer is somewhere in the building."

"But the killer doesn't know we're here. It's like cat and mouse, and we're the cat. Let's go find our mouse."

The key they'd made worked perfectly. Chelsea let out a breath she hadn't realized she'd been holding as the light to the Communication Room blinked on.

She looked around the room. It was hard to believe her life had changed so much since she'd last been there. It seemed as though the room should have transformed somehow, but it was the same. The whine of the machines, the barrier of sandbags, the steady hum of the cooler, the painted concrete, the fire extinguisher nozzles on the ceiling . . .

"Hello—Chelsea, are you in there?" Amber waved her hand in front of Chelsea's face.

"Sorry. I was just thinking." She shook her head, trying to focus. Chelsea led Amber to a putty-colored printer. Reams of paper were stacked behind it, in accordion pleats.

"This is the record of every call made from one of the businesses here—let's see, it's called Oxford Stock Brokerage. This stack is just from the day before yesterday. That's the beauty of the Smythe Towers Intelligent Building System. Once we load Diane's number, we'll be able to print out every call she made. We'll need to look for a number she called a lot, especially internal calls. Anything inside Smythe Towers."

Amber tumbled into a swivel chair and sat with her arms on the chair arms, head back, eyes closed. Twisting from side to side, she asked, "Do you know how to work that computer? Have you tried to do it before?"

"Nope!" Chelsea said, her voice artificially bright. She patted Amber's shoulder and added, "But I know it can be done. I'm just not exactly sure how. Nola explained it to me, and I have notes around here somewhere. Wait." Squeezing her eyes shut, she moaned, "Oh, no."

"What?"

"This system is set up to bill calls that go *out* of the building. Like long-distance calls. I don't think it prints calls made inside, from office to office."

"Wonderful," Amber groaned. "That's the information we need."

"There must be a way to get at the data. Nola said *every* call is recorded, but nobody's interested in office-to-office calls because there's no charge. But she did say there is a record. Let me see what I can do. . . ."

Amber shook her head. "You've always been terrible at technical things. Face it, if you try to work this computer, we don't have a prayer. Give me the notes. Do you have a manual somewhere?"

"On that desk." Trotting over to the desk, Chelsea picked up the clipboard and scrawled numbers at the bottom of the yellow page. "Okay. Diane's office was room 2231. Her phone number was 555-5523. You'll need that. Now, I bet there are instructions to access internal calls. Here you go." She handed the clipboard to Amber. From a side drawer she retrieved a computer manual and dropped it in front of her friend with a thud. "Thanks, Amber. It's all yours."

"Between your notes and the book, I think maybe I might be able to do it. Just don't touch the keyboard."

Chelsea smiled. Amber did know her well. She'd barely understood Nola's simple instructions, and would be lost trying to change the menu. Amber was at home with technology. Let her deal with it.

Raking her fingers through her hair, Amber leaned close to the screen and squinted. She began to peck at keys. She stopped, then pecked again. "This'll take me a while, Chels. Why don't you go and try the goat? I know it's a long shot, but it's better than nothing. I'm just going to need the right access. . . ."

"Okay. I guess it's worth a try." Chelsea unwrapped the wires from the goat and rolled a secretary's chair to the wall containing the phone lines. Behind her, she heard the *click-click* sound of Amber tapping the computer keys. Dropping into her chair, Chelsea sat heavy, motionless. Why were her emotions so uneven? The banter with Amber had been light, but that was all it was, a thin coating of words so that what they were doing would feel normal. The goat dangled from her fingertips as she stared, trying to visualize where she'd been sitting when they'd hooked onto the Dover call.

In front of her, plastic nubs marched from floor to ceiling in rows like tiny gravestones. Had she been sitting to the right? To the left? She shook her head. It was impossible.

"Chelsea. Chelsea! *Be* the goat," Amber called out. "Do not use your eyes. Let the Force guide you."

"Don't quit your day job," Chelsea answered over her shoulder. She knew Amber was trying to get her to relax, but she felt tight. She was going to dive into the very thing that had brought her to Diane's body. Instead of the thrill she'd felt when she'd listened before, her stomach knit on itself. Somewhere in that tangle of colors was the line she needed. There was nothing to do but plunge in. Taking a deep breath, she grounded one wire, then clipped onto a powder blue line. She pressed the handset to her ear.

A woman described a mutual fund transfer to a man who could only manage to say, *"Uh-huh, uh-huh, uh-huh, uh-huh"* in short, staccato bursts.

She unhooked the clip, then tried again. This line was empty. She tried a third, then a fourth. Clip, listen, pull. Clip, listen, pull.

"No luck, huh?" Amber called absently.

"Nope."

"I'm sorry this is taking me so long. It's pretty complicated. . . ."

Clipping on, Chelsea heard a string of women's voices, but no man's voice. Nine more empty lines, then two filled with the tart notes of no-nonsense businesswomen. Another empty. This is impossible, she thought. She hooked onto what she thought was just another business line, and was about to unhook it when she heard her name.

"Did you hear the story about Chelsea Smythe?" a woman asked. *"I heard it was the Smythe girl who led the police on that goose chase. The article didn't say a whole lot—"*

"It was in the paper? Where? I missed it."

"Section A, page 26. And guess how she got the information? By eavesdropping on the Smythe Towers phone lines."

"Are you serious? How could she do that?"

"I don't know. The article didn't say exactly how, it just said she was listening in."

"The little twit!"

"No kidding. Anyway, the police were here this morning looking for Diane in her office. And get this—she still hasn't showed up."

"Unbelievable! Do you think she's dead?"

"Me? No." There was a sound, like a sip from a coffee mug, and then, "Well . . . I don't know. That one did what she wanted when she wanted to. I think she could be anywhere—I mean, she slipped in and out of her office like a spider. And I'll tell you something else—if she knew she was bringing grief to John Smythe, she might stay hid in Mexico for the rest of her life and let him rot. They used to be as tight as they come, but then, bango! Start the fireworks!"

"Was he cheating? It's usually the man that cheats."

"That I don't know, and far be it from me to repeat anything I'm not sure of. I've followed their whole romance from the start. I was there when they met."

"Really?"

"Oh, yes. It was an office party. Diane just sort of slid up to him and purred. The old boy didn't know what hit him."

A cough, and then a chuckle. "I swear, this is better

than reading the National Enquirer. Young, sexy lawyer disappears, but no body shows up. Is she hiding out? Is she dead?"

A harsh laugh, then, *"Dead like Elvis. Maybe yes, maybe no."*

"You're just two doors down from Diane, right? Have you seen her?"

"Not in a long time. A couple weeks ago, when I was leaving to go home, I heard some pretty loud voices coming from behind closed doors. Sounded like she was arguing pretty hot with some man. I can tell you, she was a dangerous sort of person. Lived right on the edge."

Little drafts of cool air swept over her, but Chelsea felt hot. Her heart began to pound.

"You know what I think? If Diane is missing, then it's a shame for John Smythe. His first wife died, you know. Talk about lightning striking twice."

"My God!" the woman gasped. *"I thought he was just divorced! The first wife died? I always figured Smythe was like all the rest and traded his first wife in for a younger model."*

"Nope. There was some sort of car wreck years

ago. The kid's from that marriage. It's probably the shock of her mamma's death that warped that child. Listening in on the phone lines—that's as low as peeking through windows. The little sneak, I'd like to wring her—"

A hand pressed down on Chelsea's shoulder. Chelsea jumped, turned, spun the goat away from the wall.

"What's the matter, Chels? I was watching you— you've turned gray."

"Nothing," Chelsea whispered. Two women, women she didn't know, were laughing at her. At her family.

"Tell me what happened. Did you find the voice?" Amber asked.

"No. I—I heard some women—they were talking about me and Diane. It sounds like what happened is all over the office."

"How?" Amber cried.

"They said our story was in the paper."

"The *newspaper*? You've got to be joking! I can't even *believe* it!"

Chelsea slumped in her chair. Spurts of heat raced through her head. Phrases like "Diane might stay hid

158

in Mexico and let him rot," and "the little sneak. That's as low as peeking through windows" played themselves over and over again.

"Listen, Chelsea, this could be bad. I can't believe people already know about Diane. About us being up in Dover Cave. About the goat. What did they say?"

"I don't know. Things. My—my throat feels dry."

"You're just stressed. Listen, I'll get you a drink. Would you like that?"

Chelsea nodded.

"Good. A shot of sugar should do the trick, because you really look like you're going to pass out. Have you eaten anything since yesterday?"

"Not much. A Coke sounds great. Thanks."

Amber put her face right next to Chelsea's, as if she were a coach staring down a player. "The drink machines are off the lobby, right? Down that first hallway?"

Chelsea nodded again.

"I'll only be a minute. Now, when I come back, I'll knock twice, wait, then knock once. Three knocks. It's a code. That way, you'll know it's me. Stay off that stupid goat till I get back." She grabbed her purse, opened the door, checked quickly around, and slipped out.

The rumble of machinery pulsed the air. Chelsea rubbed her eyes and stood. The best thing she could do now would be to work. Walking to Amber's desk, she stared at the computer screens, at the rows of green numbers that seemed to roll to infinity.

Suddenly, a ribbon of highlight began to move across the bottom of the screen. Someone was sending her a message through the Smythe Towers electronic mail. The string of letters tapped onto the computer, like a mother duck leading her young. Letter by letter, it spelled a message.

I KNOW YOU ARE DOWN THERE. DO NOT TALK TO ANYONE. DO NOT GO TO THE POLICE. DO NOT USE THE GOAT. I'VE GOT NOTHING TO LOSE, CHELSEA. I'LL BE WATCHING YOU.

A small cry escaped from her mouth. Or was it a scream? She was frozen. Ice clamped her muscles, her tissues. The string of words seared her brain, as she read them over, again and again.

I KNOW YOU ARE DOWN THERE. DO NOT TALK TO ANYONE. DO NOT GO TO THE POLICE. DO NOT USE THE GOAT.

I'VE GOT NOTHING TO LOSE, CHELSEA. I'LL BE WATCHING YOU.

No sound, no motion, save the tiny pulse of light the cursor beat on the screen.

Two thuds. A pause, then one more.

And then, like a whisper, the message blinked off the screen, and Chelsea was, once again, alone.

11

They came again. Two knocks, a pause, then another knock. The code. Somewhere in her mind, Chelsea put together the thought. What if it was the man? What if, when she opened the door, she stared straight into the barrel of a gun? Her only protection was the metal door, and yet, the message had come to her inside the room. She wasn't safe here. There was no place safe, inside or out.

Two knocks, a pause, then another knock. This time, they sounded more insistent. Chelsea moved to the door. Pressing her mouth to the doorjamb, she cried, "Who's there?"

"It's me. Amber." The voice was muffled. "Remember the code?"

Opening the door a sliver, Chelsea saw Amber's middle. She opened the door the rest of the way, and Amber stepped inside.

"Chelsea, what's the matter with you?"

"We're leaving."

"But—"

Chelsea grabbed her by the arm. She didn't mean to press her nails into the fleshy part of Amber's arm, didn't mean to squeeze until she saw a flicker of pain cross Amber's eyes, but Chelsea's own body had stopped obeying her.

Breathe! she commanded herself. Keep it together. Stay calm! But her body began to shake as terror surged through her. Words flashed behind her eyes, one after another.

He knows who you are. He knows your name. He knows you're here. Maybe he can see you. Maybe he can hear you. He knows who you are. He knows your name.

"We're leaving," she repeated to Amber. "Now." Her throat tightened. She sucked in a shivery gulp of air.

"Okay, Chelsea. Okay."

Through the shadowy blocks of cars Chelsea ran, jerking like a rabbit being chased by hounds. Behind her, Amber followed, still clutching the cans of Coke, and Chelsea became suddenly furious at how slowly Amber moved. Keep up, or get out of my way, Chelsea mentally screamed at Amber. Hurry! Move! I won't get killed because you're slow!

A man sat, fumbling for his keys in the front seat of his Mercury. He glanced up at them, then looked away. Was he the killer, Chelsea asked herself? Was he just pretending to be starting his car? Was he watching her? The man looked up, and his eyes didn't focus on her or Amber. He was engrossed in something else. The car started and he eased out, then drove away. Somehow Chelsea knew he wasn't the one.

"Wait, Chelsea!" Amber puffed. "Do you want me to drive?"

"No. Just get in the car."

Tires squealing, she backed out, then sped toward

the exit. Away from Smythe Towers. Toward the light. Outside, the world looked just as it always had, and it surprised Chelsea. The external world went on moving without any acknowledgment of what had happened in one of its dark corners.

"We're gone now. So you can tell me, what happened?"

"There was a message that came up on the computer screen. It said, 'I know who you are, Chelsea. I know you're down there. Don't go to the police. Don't use the goat. Don't tell anyone.'"

The pink drained from Amber's face. "The man knows we were there? My God! How?" And then, after a pause, "Are you sure?"

"Yes! Of course I'm sure. What do you think I am, crazy?"

"That's not what I—"

"Because, that's what it would mean! If those words weren't on the screen, if I thought I saw the message but it really wasn't there . . . it would mean I was mentally gone." It was too hard to drive. Chelsea turned into an alleyway. "I can't be, can I? You know me,

Amber—am I . . . crazy?" She looked at Amber, begging her to believe. Shaking, because the answer to the question meant so much, she asked again, "I need to know. Do you think I've lost my mind?"

"No. Someone's playing with your head. Don't let them."

Chelsea pressed her hands against her eyes. No tears, she commanded herself. But they slipped through her fingers and down her cheeks, dropping quietly into her lap. "Thank you, Amber." Her voice was husky. "Thank you for believing me."

Amber's face turned suddenly hard. "I think we have to go to the police. Fayette and Beech need to know what's happened."

"No!" Chelsea groaned. "The message said not to talk to anyone. It said not to talk to the police! No!"

"I know what you're saying, Chelsea, but if the killer says we shouldn't go to the police, then that's exactly what we should do. Don't you see? We must have hit a nerve. There's one thing Beech said that I still think is right: We can't be the ones who decide which information is important. We've got to tell them everything that's happening."

"Oh! Sure!" Chelsea flared. "Your name wasn't on that message! It said *Chelsea*. What's it to you? You're not the one who might get killed—"

"I'm in this with you all the way. And don't you dare turn on me now."

"Maybe we should go to my dad. . . ."

"We can call him from the station. I don't even want to stop to make a call. There's no safe place for us except the police station, Chelsea. As long as he knows who we are, and we don't know who he is, we're sitting ducks."

Amber reached over to give her a hard squeeze.

"I'm scared," Chelsea said softly. "I'm really, really scared."

"I know. But someone is trying to freak you out. He, or they, are counting on the fact that you'll fold under pressure. But we can't. We've got to try to stay tough."

It was three o'clock, and the police station was busier than it had been when they'd last walked inside. A man dressed in uniform looked up and asked, "What do you need, ladies?"

167

"We need to see Detective Fayette. I'm Amber Farrington, and this is Chelsea Smythe. He knows who we are."

"Take a seat over there." He pointed to the same orange vinyl chairs they'd sat in the first time. Normally, routine made Chelsea feel secure, but nothing could feel normal about this.

"Can I use your phone?" Chelsea asked.

"Sure. What number?"

Chelsea gave her father's number, and the officer punched it in and handed her the phone. With her peripheral vision, Chelsea saw a look of surprise wash across Amber's face.

"You're calling your father? Now?"

Chelsea nodded. "He needs to know what happened. I—I want him down here with me."

"Smythe Towers," a cool voice on the other end of the line said.

"This is Chelsea Smythe. Could you please put me through to my father?"

"One moment."

"Chelsea?" Her father's voice came on the line. "I

was hoping you would call. How are you feeling? I thought I'd let you sleep, so I didn't—"

"Daddy? I'm at the police station again. Something's happened."

Her father's tone immediately changed. "What's the matter? Are you all right?"

"No."

"Are you injured? Have you been in an accident?"

"I—we're—I need you!" A sob broke from her. The officer silently handed her a box of tissues, then turned and busied himself with paperwork.

"Listen, sweetheart, I'll be right there. Ten minutes, and I'll be there. Just hold on."

Chelsea swallowed hard. She needed to pull herself together. Better to tell him the hard part over the telephone, so she wouldn't have to see his face. "Wait, Daddy? I—I've got to tell you something. I . . ." Her words tightened to a whisper. "I took your keys. To Smythe Towers. I was in the Communication Room today—"

Without hesitating, he said, "Don't worry about it. We'll settle it later. Just ten minutes, Chelsea. I'm on my way. I'm going to hang up now, and then I'll be there."

"Okay. Good-bye. Please hurry."

A click, and then a dial tone. Amber pulled the phone from Chelsea's grasp and handed it to the officer.

"Just take a seat over there," the officer said gently. "Detective Fayette will be with you in a moment."

Amber put her hand on Chelsea's shoulder. "What did he say?"

"He said he's on his way. He's coming." Chelsea's heart began to feel even again. She took in a few wavering breaths, then sat down on an orange chair.

Only a few minutes passed when a side door opened and Fayette motioned to them. "Ladies. I feel honored! Beech is off today, but I'm here, and delighted to see you both. Please, come into my office."

This time, Fayette had on brown slacks and a tie the color of cinnamon toast. They followed him down the hall, turning automatically into his office. A half-eaten doughnut lay on a paper plate at the edge of his desk.

"Would you like one?" he asked, pointing to the limp doughnut.

When they shook their heads no, he took a sip of coffee, swallowed, then leaned back and placed his hands behind his head. "Well, ladies, I must admit, I am intrigued. What brings you back this time? Did you find the body of Jimmy Hoffa?"

"No," Amber answered tartly.

"Oh. Well, you can't blame a guy for hoping. So, what's up?"

"We went to Smythe Towers today. We were down in the Communication Room, and Chelsea got this . . . message. We thought we should tell you about it."

Chelsea shifted in her seat. She hated dealing with him, but whom else could she go to? He was the detective who knew the case.

"I was in the Communication Room—," Chelsea began.

"Listening in with that goat thing? Were you doing that again?"

"Yes."

"I thought I already told you girls, you can't go eavesdropping on other people's conversations. It's against the law. I could arrest you both. Did you get this . . . message . . . from using that goat?"

"No."

Fayette made a steeple with his fingers. "Good. Before we go on, let's get something straight, ladies. You cannot use that goat to help with this investigation. It won't do a thing for our case, so don't even try."

"But, what about—"

Fayette held up his hand. "Even if you heard your mystery man saying he'd killed fifteen nuns and stashed them in his basement—at this point, I couldn't use it. It's poison."

"Poison?" Amber crinkled her forehead.

"Look, the first time you listened in on that man's conversation, you were a citizen who presumably didn't know any better. But remember how I told you using that thing was against the law?"

Both Amber and Chelsea nodded.

"Try to follow me now. We have, in law enforcement, a policy that states that any fruit from a poison tree is poison, too. I'm trying to explain a principle here. See, the police can't just go around listening in on conversations. We need a court order for that." Narrowing his eyes, he pointed a long finger toward the door and said, "Say that if, all on my own, I decided Joe Schmoe over there was selling cocaine. Say I borrowed your goat to get information to nail him. The whole case would be thrown out of court."

"Why?" Amber asked.

"Because using the goat is illegal. That's the poison tree. If I heard Joe Schmoe tell some druggie that he had three tons stashed in his garage, and I went to his house and sure enough, there were three tons of cocaine packed up to his ceiling, it wouldn't matter. The information came from the poison tree. The cocaine itself would be the poison fruit off that poison tree."

"That doesn't make any sense," Chelsea countered. "I mean, if the man is guilty, then he's guilty."

"Guilty, yes. But I'm trying to get you to see that I couldn't take him to court. Not on a bet. I would have obtained my evidence *illegally*. Therefore, in the eyes of the law, the evidence would not exist. Poison fruit. Do you understand what I'm saying?"

"Yes. But I don't get what it has to do with Amber and me."

Fayette sighed. "At this point, any lawyer worth his

or her beans would stand up in court and tell the judge that we, the police, put you two up to using that thing. No matter what you overheard, the judge would throw the case out so fast your head would spin like the little girl in *The Exorcist*. Poison fruit. So, just stop listening in with that goat thing. It could get you ladies into trouble, and it won't do anybody any good. Agreed?"

"Fine," Chelsea said. "But this message didn't come from the goat. It came from the computer."

"The computer?" Fayette tapped his chin.

"Yes," Amber added. "It was a threat, made to Chelsea. Somebody typed her a message to scare her."

"Wait a minute. Before we go any further, I'm going to flip on the tape recorder. Is that okay?"

"Sure," Amber said, shrugging.

When he saw the expression on Chelsea's face, he said, "This little tape recorder isn't going to hurt you, Ms. Smythe. It's just going to sit there, turning around and around and around. Now, that shouldn't bother you, should it?"

"I guess not." For some reason, it *did* bother her. She hated the way the tape recorder made her feel. It was the same way she felt about writing letters; whatever she said was there, on paper, permanent. If it were wrong, she couldn't take it back and explain. It was out in the universe, forever. A tape recorder would mean whatever came out of her mouth would live apart from her on that thin ribbon of tape. She felt herself squirm.

"It's just there to help me in case I forget." He pursed his lips. "All right?"

"I guess," Chelsea reluctantly agreed.

"Fine. Fine." Fayette pushed two buttons on a dented tape recorder. "Now then, let's get down to business. Tell me about this message."

Clearing her throat, Chelsea found herself leaning into the tape recorder, as if she were giving a recitation at a school play.

"Okay. I was sitting in the Communication Room," she said, a little too loudly.

"That's all right," Fayette interrupted. "This microphone picks up real good. Just talk to me."

Chelsea swallowed. Moderating her voice so that it sounded almost normal, she began again. "Like I said,

I was in the Communication Room, and I was using the goat. I know I shouldn't have, but, I was trying to find the man."

"Okay. You were snooping with the goat. Then what happened?"

Chelsea blew air out between her lips. She decided to edit out the next part about what she'd heard on the goat and go straight to the message on the computer. Fayette didn't need to know everything. "I got thirsty. Amber left to get me a Coke. I went to the computer, and I saw this . . . message. It came on, one letter at a time. And it said . . ." Her voice caught.

"That's okay. Take your time."

"It said, 'I know you're down there. Don't go to the police. I'll be watching you.'"

Amber leaned forward eagerly. "And it typed, 'I've got nothing to lose, Chelsea.' It wrote her name! And it said, 'Do not use the goat.' Chelsea forgot to say that part."

"Is that correct?" Fayette zeroed in on Chelsea's eyes.

"Yes," Chelsea nodded. "It scared me to death. I mean, it had to be that man. The man with the gravelly voice. He's somewhere in the building, and he knew

176

my name. He knew I was down there. It totally freaked me."

"And me," Amber added.

Fayette broke his gaze and turned to Amber. "But, Amber, you weren't in the Communication Room at this point. At the time the message came on the screen. Correct?"

"That's right," Amber said, nodding. "But I came right after, and Chelsea looked as white as a sheet. When she told me about what happened, I said, 'Chelsea, we've got to tell the police.' So here we are."

"That's very good, Amber." Fayette tapped his knuckle on the desktop. "So, let's get back to this computer thing. The screen had a message that told you not to come here? And it typed out your name?"

"Yes."

"How is that possible?"

"We have a modem in our building. Anyone in Smythe Towers can send a message to anyone else."

"Do you think there might be a mob connection?" Amber broke in. "Maybe Diane got mixed up with the Mafia. Maybe they were the ones who killed her."

Fayette snorted. "The mob? You've been sitting in

movie theaters too long. Diane isn't involved with any mob. We've checked this thing out far enough to know that."

"It was just a theory," Amber stammered. "I was trying to help. We've been trying to do this on our own. No one even believed Chelsea."

Fayette gave her a sharp look. "That's not necessarily true. We initially had our doubts, I'll admit. But things have changed. We think something's *definitely* going on."

"Really?" Chelsea felt a wave of relief. The police were finally listening.

"Have you found anything?" Amber asked.

"Well, we've been to Diane's new condo. All of her belongings are there, including photographs and her clothing. Things people normally take when they leave for good. We've left messages on her phones asking her to call in. We've run a check to see if we could find any charges she might have made on her credit cards. Nada. It's getting close to twenty-four hours, girls. With every minute that goes by, we're getting more and more interested in your body story. In fact"—he hesitated, then looked sternly at Chelsea—"I'll tell you just how seriously we're taking this. I sent a crew up to Dover Lake. They've been dragging for her body since early this morning."

"What?" Chelsea gasped.

"Stands to reason that if someone hid a body in a cave by a lake, their plan was to dump that body in the water. Put a couple weights on it, throw it overboard, and they think they're home free."

Chelsea's heart jostled in her chest.

"Now, let's get back to the message. This message not only had your name, but it told you *not* to use the goat? Correct?"

"Yes."

"I've got a question. Would a regular person at Smythe Towers know about the goat? Just your average customer that worked in one of your run-of-the-mill offices?"

"I—I don't know," Chelsea said.

"Before this morning, when it came out in the paper, was your ability to eavesdrop on other people's conversations common knowledge at Smythe Towers?" Fayette leaned forward over his desk and looked at her searchingly.

"No. I just started in the Communication Room. How could anyone really know?"

"So someone in the building typed you a threatening message. Have you talked to your father about this?" Fayette kept his comments directed at Chelsea.

"I called him from here. He's on his way." Chelsea looked at the floor. The tiles were the color of dirty sand. Or was it a white floor that had just grayed with time?

"Were you working today? I mean, did you punch in on a clock or something?"

"No one at Smythe Towers, except maybe the maintenance people, punches in," Chelsea said. "It's not that kind of building."

"Ooooh."

Chelsea flushed. She hadn't meant it to sound that way.

"But your dad was working at Smythe Towers today. Correct?" Another question aimed at Chelsea.

"Yes."

"What time did he leave for work this morning?"

"Early. I think—I'm not sure. I was asleep."

"Is he still at Smythe Towers?" Fayette seemed to

be laying down his sentences like a bricklayer laid brick. One row, then another.

"He's on his way here. I told you, I called."

"Has your dad had any . . . financial problems lately?"

"No!"

"How far along is the divorce between him and Diane? Is it final yet?"

"I don't think so."

"Interesting." The phone rang. Fayette straightened and snapped off the record button. As he picked up the phone, he watched Chelsea, never once taking his eyes off her.

Then Chelsea knew. From the way he looked at her, without him saying the words, she knew. When he hung up the phone, he tried to make his voice sound as gentle as possible. It didn't help. Every word was an agony.

"That was the crew at Dover Lake. I'm sorry to be the one to tell you. They found Diane's body."

12

"Your father is here," Fayette said. "Amber, why don't you and I leave the room. Let's give these folks some privacy."

As they rose, Amber placed a hand on Chelsea's forearm.

It's all right, Chelsea told her with her eyes. Don't worry. I can handle it. They'd been with Fayette for what seemed like hours since the call came about Diane. Questions, and then more questions. Chelsea knew her father should have arrived, but she was forced to wait while Fayette grilled her endlessly about things she'd already said.

Finally, a knock on the door. Her father was there.

Amber and Fayette disappeared, pushing past Chelsea's father as they went.

And then it was her father, holding her, hugging her as if he'd fall if she weren't there to hold him up.

"She's dead!" he said into her hair. He rocked her back and forth, repeating it over and over again. "They told me when I arrived. They found her body. In Dover Lake. Who would do this? It's senseless." He sagged in her arms.

"Sit down, Daddy."

She led him in front of Fayette's desk, where he collapsed into the chair Amber had been sitting in. "I can't believe it! Diane! Dead! Really . . . gone! I keep seeing her, and I wish we hadn't left it so badly. The last time I saw her—" He punched his leg and let out a hoarse, raking sob.

"It's going to be okay." Chelsea stroked the back of his shoulder. She'd never seen her father cry this way before, with such anguish. Maybe he had when her real mother died, but she didn't remember. A helpless feeling seeped through her. What should she do? How could she comfort him? With his head bowed, she saw scalp shining through his once thick hair. His hair was thinner than she remembered. What a crazy thing to think of, especially now. But her mind went through a strange inventory as her father choked on tears: one feature for each stroke of her hand.

The skin around his neck—crinkled in a tiny network of lines. Had it been that way before? Hands—weathered. Veins the size of blue ropes, ready to pop from underneath his skin. Tiniest stubble of a beard: gray. A gray beard? When had his beard turned so gray?

He looked up at her, his face lined with pain that made his features old. Brusquely, he rubbed out the tears that had dampened his face. He took a deep breath. "I'm sorry. I'm sure it's very disconcerting to see your father cry."

"No, Daddy. It isn't. Really." She paused, searching for words. "Would you be bothered to see me cry?" She dropped into her chair and faced her father.

"Of course not. But neither one of us ever does."

"It'd probably be good for both of us if we did," she

said, pressing her face into his neck. "I saw it on a talk show once—they said the whole world would be better off if everyone cried together once in a while. Or maybe it was just a Kleenex commercial."

She was talking nonsense, but she was trying to cheer him, trying to break the mask of pain on his face. When she pulled away, he made a faint attempt at a smile that vanished as quickly as it appeared.

"What happened to you today? In the Communication Room? They told me you were threatened—"

"When did they tell you that? You were supposed to come in here the second you arrived. I've been watching the clock, worried that you were in an accident!"

"I've been at the station for quite a while now. They asked me questions. But I want to hear from you what happened. Tell me, please."

"It's not important. Not right now."

He took her hand and pressed it into his. "I need to know."

"I got a message on the modem. It told me to stay away. Whoever wrote it knew my name. He knew I was down there."

Her father paled. "Then the killer is in the building."

"I know."

"I should have believed you," he said quietly. "I should have protected you. I'm sorry, Chelsea." He squeezed her hand until it burned. An expression of sadness, mixed with anger, clouded his face. "Sweetheart . . . this is hard for me. But there's something you should know."

The way he said it, the way he looked at her, made her stomach clench.

"They—the police—are searching my car. It's okay," he said, holding up his hand. "I gave them permission. It's just that they think that . . . I find this so difficult that I can hardly say it. They think I might have been involved in Diane's death."

"Involved!" Chelsea spit the word.

"The phone call you overheard. With the goat. They believe you were listening to . . . me."

"What! That's absurd! Don't they think I know my own father's voice! How stupid do they think I am? It was a man—a man with a gravelly voice. Not *your* voice. What are they? A group of morons? What—if they—" She stopped. She couldn't find more words to put to the rage that churned inside her. Rage and . . .

guilt. Her father was being dragged through a ridiculous process, all because she'd listened in on a call she never should have heard. She'd started it, but she couldn't stop it. Chelsea cursed herself silently.

"Calm down. I have nothing to hide. In a way, my worst fear was that Diane might have just disappeared, and we'd never know anything for sure. But now, the detectives can go on and find out what really happened to her."

"How did she die? Could they tell?"

"Nothing conclusive. They told me her arms and legs had been strapped with weights. If you hadn't heard what you did, and gone up there to the cave . . . she'd still be down there, at the bottom of the lake. Her body has been taken to the coroner's. They told me they found . . . trauma . . . around her head. We'll have to wait to know for sure."

His suit had pulled to one side, making him appear slightly lopsided, and tears had left dime-sized marks on his powder blue shirt. She'd never seen him so vulnerable. She'd never loved him more.

"Daddy, I need to know something." Chelsea leveled her gaze at him. There was something unreal about the way she addressed her father, as if they were suddenly on equal footing. *Daddy, I need to know something. Why haven't we been able to talk like this before? When the stakes weren't so high?* He looked at her intently.

"Why did Diane leave?"

"Now is not the time—"

"Yes it is. I've tried to do this on my own, figure out what's happened, put the pieces together, but I've just made a mess of things. Tell me what's been going on."

Her father dropped his head. He sighed deeply. "I suppose I should have told you from the start, Chelsea. But, I just wanted to . . . forget. It happened the night she left. I found Diane's bank statement. There was over a million and a half dollars in that one account."

"What!" Chelsea was stunned. "A *million and a half dollars*! How? I mean, where—"

"I don't know." He looked up at her. "It wasn't from me. I confronted her when she came home that night. I told her I knew whatever she was doing had to be illegal. I said no lawyer that dealt with petty claims could generate that kind of money."

"What did she say?"

"She told me to turn a blind eye. She said what I didn't know wouldn't hurt me. I told her that was ridiculous, that I was her husband and I had a right to understand what was going on. When I told her I loved her, but would not stand for anything that was illegal, or immoral, she said I was an old man who didn't understand the way the world worked, and I had a choice. Leave it, or she would leave me. That's what she said, as cold as ice. She didn't cry. She didn't apologize. She just stared. I chose the latter."

"Oh, Daddy."

"I ordered her to go, right then. I told her she was not to even set foot in Smythe Towers. It was my building, and I said I didn't want any of her sins to taint my business. I told her I'd call the police and tell them everything if I ever found her back there. Since then, I've heard rumors that she'd slipped in and out of the building, but . . . I never saw her again."

"Why didn't you tell me? I could have handled it."

"I see that now, but . . . I thought I'd already lost you." He began to choke. "I wasn't sure who you loved more. I was . . . afraid she'd tell you lies. Afraid you'd believe her. Afraid you'd leave me, too."

189

"You're my father," Chelsea said. She clung to him, feeling his warmth. How could she have been so stupid? How could he not understand the way she felt about him? Or hadn't she been sure herself? It had been so confusing. They'd drifted apart, until he'd become a cardboard figure, nothing more. Mistake! Mistake after mistake after mistake. "I love you," she whispered. "More than anything."

There was a loud knock and the door was flung open. Detective Fayette and a uniformed officer filled the doorway. Fayette's curly white hair framed his face like a snug-fitting cap. He looked grave.

"What is it?" her father asked.

"We ran a check on your wife's accounts, looking for activity. One of the reports shows that your soon-to-be ex-wife had a bank balance of close to two million dollars. Once the divorce was final, you would have gotten nothing. Quite a motive for murder."

"That's ridiculous!" her father cried. "I have plenty of money. I don't need any more from her or anyone."

"Have you seen these before?" Fayette held up a Ziplock Baggie. Even from across the room, Chelsea could see the sparkle. The shape. Diamond studs. Diane's diamond earrings.

"These were found under the floor mat of your car. Do you know who they belong to?"

"They look like my wife's," her father said slowly.

"They look exactly like the earrings Chelsea described seeing in Diane's ears when she found her body in the cave. Are these the ones, Chelsea?"

"I don't know," she stammered.

"There's blood on one of them. And a strand of hair. We believe it to be the blood and hair of Diane Smythe. We'll run a DNA analysis, but I think we both know what it'll say."

Her father stared, numb.

Fayette gave the officer a tiny nod. The officer went over to where they sat. With an arm under her father's elbow, he helped him stand.

"John Smythe, you are hereby arrested for the murder of Diane Hutton Smythe," Fayette began. "You have the right to remain silent."

"No!" Chelsea screamed.

"Wait. Please!" Something in the way her father

said it made the whole room freeze. "Before you go any further, I have to tell my daughter something." He turned, and looked straight into Chelsea's eyes. "I didn't do this, sweetheart. Do you hear me? I didn't do this. Please, don't panic. Innocent people don't go to jail. Now, I want you to stay with Amber until I get out of here. Don't stay in the house alone. Understand?"

"Mr. Smythe—"

"A moment. Is that too much to ask?!"

Fayette fell silent. Her father turned back to her. "Do not go to Smythe Towers. The killer is in there. Promise me you'll stay away."

"Daddy—," Chelsea wailed.

"Promise!" His face flashed with the old authority. "I want the keys. Give me the keys you took from my desk. I do not want you in the Communication Room."

"Give him the keys, Chelsea," Fayette ordered.

Chelsea reached onto the floor and pulled up her purse. With shaking hands, she rifled the contents until her fingers grasped the cold jagged metal of keys. She pressed them into her father's hand.

"Good." Her father forced a smile. "I love you, darling. Don't worry. Everything's going to turn out just fine."

The officer took the keys and pulled her father's hands behind his back. Fayette began to read the rights again, from the beginning, and over his voice Chelsea heard a sound that she knew was the worst sound she would ever hear in her life. The sound of handcuffs being snapped onto her father's wrists.

13

The house was empty. Chelsea set down her purse and flipped on the lights. To her left, the living room: furniture, smooth and polished, peppered with light from their large chandelier. To the right, the dining room, with a huge vase of orange tiger lilies bursting from a crystal centerpiece. Her shoes created a hollow tapping sound along the stone as she made her way to the kitchen. Had her footsteps always echoed when she walked? Funny, in the past she remembered a sound, but never an echo. She kicked off her shoes and walked the rest of the way in her socks. The black-

and-white tile of the kitchen floor felt cold.

Sitting at the counter, she stared out the large bay window as scenes from the police station drifted through her mind. Her father, being led away. Fayette. Amber. She sighed. She was going to have to pack, to fold her life into a suitcase and leave for the Farringtons' home. Lucky she had a place to go. In the beginning, she hadn't been too sure.

When she'd first seen Amber's mother, Mrs. Farrington had been seated next to Amber in the foyer of the police station. She looked like a tropical jungle in her bright, splashy print pantsuit and large wooden earrings. Everything about Mrs. Farrington was big. Her voice, her laugh; it had always seemed to Chelsea as if Amber's mother were a television set with the volume turned all the way up. From across the room, she'd watched as Mrs. Farrington clucked over Amber, stroking her hair and touching her cheek. Her mother seemed to be in an excited state. She gestured with her hands, making grand, sweeping motions; she seemed to be talking a lot.

Chelsea's temple began to pulse. What would Mrs. Farrington do when she saw Chelsea? Would she be angry? Furious that her daughter had been dragged into something so unsavory? Would she begin to yell, so that all the people in the station would stop what they were doing to watch the scene?

Chelsea, your father is a murderer. Stay away from my daughter! Stay away from all of us!

Mrs. Farrington looked up and caught Chelsea's eye. Although she was heavy, she moved with surprising speed.

"Chelsea!"

She'd jumped up, racing across the room, hugging Chelsea into her soft breasts until Chelsea felt the breath squeeze from her.

"I've heard what's happened, you poor darling. It's a travesty, an absolute travesty. You must be devastated. But, I promise, everything will be fine. Your father's already called Anthony Gionni, the best attorney in the state, and I understand he'll be here within the hour." She'd pulled apart, searching Chelsea's face. "Now, listen, Chelsea. It might look bad, but we trust your father. We *know* he didn't have anything to do with this . . . tragedy. Your car's here, right?"

"Yes."

"I insist you go home, pack whatever you need, and then drive over to our house and stay with us. We've got a lovely guest room sitting empty. You're welcome for as long as you need. We've missed seeing you so much, and Amber thinks so much of you, Chelsea. We all do."

"Thanks," Chelsea had said. "Thank you."

Amber had been hovering behind her mother. Stepping forward awkwardly, she'd whispered into Chelsea's ear. "It's going to be okay. I promise. I'm going to leave now so I can get things ready at my house. Come over as soon as you can."

How long would she be in exile at the Farringtons'? Chelsea asked herself now. Everything had been ripped from her, and now she was being forced from her home.

"I need to pack," she told herself, half out loud. But she didn't move.

The earrings. Those were Diane's earrings. She was sure of it. Alone, the thoughts she wouldn't let herself think came bubbling up, one by one, until her mind began to boil. If Diane's earrings were in his car, then . . . then maybe . . . No! she screamed at herself, but the voice inside went on.

Maybe he did *kill Diane. Maybe he's been lying. To you. About everything. Maybe you don't know him. Maybe Diane was good and he was bad.*

Stop! She commanded her mind to think of something else. Pack! Think about packing! Make a list. What would she need? Her suitcase was in the basement. One suitcase? No, two. She might be there awhile. Her toothbrush, and her . . . She saw her father's hand, holding a club, smashing Diane's head. One blow, and then another. She saw him dragging Diane's body to the cave. Dumping her into the water. Like a movie, she saw the scene over and over again. And then the message: I KNOW YOU ARE DOWN THERE. DO NOT TALK TO ANYONE. DO NOT GO TO THE POLICE. I'VE GOT NOTHING TO LOSE, CHELSEA. I'LL BE WATCHING YOU. Her father? Had he been the one?

No. He wasn't a killer. Suspicions swirled around, damning him, but they melted against the core of faith inside her. Her father couldn't have murdered Diane. He wouldn't. He was a good man. She was sure of it.

Her eye caught the blinking of a message light on their answering machine. Something to think about.

Something normal. Rewinding the tape, she punched the button and played the messages. Voices filled the kitchen, as if life were just the same as it always had been.

"Um, Chelsea, hi! This is Todd. I was wondering about Saturday night—is seven-thirty still okay? I'll call you back soon. Oh, why don't you call me if it's not okay. I mean, if I don't hear from you, then I'll just be there. At seven-thirty. See ya."

Beep.

"Chels! I'm calling from Miami! I wish you could be here—the guys are sooooo hot. Anyway, I've sent you a letter, and *write* me, okay! Miss you."

Beep.

"Chelsea, this is your father. I've waited, hoping to let you sleep. Last night . . ." There was a pause. "I was wondering if you've got plans for this evening? If you're free, I was making a date for you with an older man. For dinner, at the restaurant of your choice. Now, don't get your expectations up, the older man is . . . me." A small laugh, and then, "Anyway, I think we need to talk more. It's one-thirty now. Call me when you can.

I'm at the office. I love you. See you tonight, I hope."

Beep, then *click, click, click.* The messages were over. Chelsea stared at the machine. Ordinary voices. Things like dates, and friends, her father. Would they ever sound easy and uncomplicated again?

The phone rang. Chelsea picked it up and cocked the receiver into her shoulder.

"Hello?"

"Chelsea. It's good to hear your voice. You're all alone in that big house, aren't you?"

Chelsea's insides contracted. "Who is this?"

"Don't you know?" asked the gravelly voice. "I thought you'd know me by now. You got my message, the one I sent you on the modem? But you went to the police. What a pity."

"Who—" Her chest became a knot of frozen breath. She couldn't go on, couldn't take the next gulp of air.

"You don't think I'm going to tell you who I am, do you? Let's just say I'm a friend of your stepmother's. God rest her soul. You've had quite a bit of fun with the goat, haven't you? Think, Chelsea, of all the trouble you'd have saved yourself if you'd only kept your nose out of other people's business. You should have listened when I sent you that message. Little girls shouldn't play with dangerous things. You've been very naughty."

"Why are you calling me?" Suddenly, a thought smashed through her. She was alone—alone in the house. Hadn't he said that? "You're all alone in that big house, aren't you?" Could he see her? Whipping around, she stared through the kitchen window. Dusk was settling over the yard. The boughs of trees trembled in the breeze, and the motion sent terror, pure and cold, straight through her. Was he out there? Watching? She searched the shadows, half expecting them to solidify into the form of a man, but they were just trees. Trees, and the beginnings of darkness.

"I have a purpose for this call. It's more than just a friendly chat. Stay out of Smythe Towers. You've tampered with things you don't understand. So far, I've managed to put out the fires you've started, but"— there was a lull, and then a warning—"that better be the end of your interference. I want to be through with you." His voice dropped a note. "You've seen what I did to your father. I can do worse things to you."

"I'll call the police," Chelsea stammered. "I'll tell them what you've said."

"Oh, please do. Tell them you've had a phone call from the mystery killer. I'm sure they'll believe you. Not that you'd have any reason to lie. You, being the daughter of an accused murderer." He took a controlled breath. "You see, your story would sound so ridiculous that I feel I can speak to you with some degree of impunity. Oh, and just in case you're planning on putting a trace on this line in the future? Don't bother. I'll never call again."

Another acrid laugh. It went through her like a shot.

"Although I must say, I feel . . . close . . . to you. I know a lot about you, Chelsea. Your room is blue, but it used to be pink. Am I right? You're a size seven. Your favorite perfume is Poison. And . . . you're too young to die."

A click, and the line went dead.

She didn't know how long she stood there. The phone, the trees, the walls, images blurred together, the voice going through her head, sparing her nothing.

She stumbled to the entryway, checked to make sure the door was securely locked, grabbed her purse, returned to the kitchen. With a quick movement, she opened her purse and removed her wallet. Fayette's card had slipped behind her driver's license. She pulled it out, punching in the numbers as fast as she could.

"Homicide." It was a woman's voice.

"I need—I need to speak to Detective Fayette."

"I'm sorry, he's gone for the day."

"Is Detective Beech in? This is an emergency."

"No. I'll put you on with our night desk. Please hold."

A moment, and then, "Night desk. Detective Baker speaking."

"This is Chelsea Smythe. My father, John Smythe, was arrested for the murder of my stepmother. Detective Fayette—"

"I know who you are. Hang on, let me get the file." A click, and Muzak swelled the line. "Hurry," Chelsea pleaded. Squeezing her eyes shut, she tried not to imagine the man, outside, staring at her through a window.

"Okay. Got it."

"I'm home alone. There was this man—"

"You're Chelsea Smythe, correct?"

The sound of her own rapid breathing was magnified in the telephone's mouthpiece. She needed to concentrate on her words. Taking a deep breath, Chelsea tried to keep her voice steady. "Yes. I'm at home. I was there, at your station, and when I got here at my house, a man—the man—the killer—called and told me to stay away from Smythe Towers. He admitted killing Diane!"

"Umm-humm. Interesting." Detective Baker paused. Chelsea could hear what sounded like paper being flipped over. It was maddening, the way he kept her suspended in the phone line's dead space.

"This wouldn't happen to be the same man that you heard before, would it? Let's see here—you described him as the man with the gravelly voice?"

"Yes! It was him!"

"He just dialed you on the phone and admitted the crime, just like that?"

"He said he killed Diane—"

"Listen, Chelsea, I think I understand what you're

204

doing. Of course you love your father—"

Chelsea banged the phone down, hard.

The killer was right. They wouldn't believe her. It just looked like a desperate attempt to get her father off the hook.

What to do? Where to turn next? The phone shrilled. Was it him? The man? She watched, numb. It rang again. Don't answer it! she commanded herself. A third ring. Then a fourth. Was he playing with her? Could she stand to hear his voice? His threats? But what if it were the police? What if they believed her? What if it were her father? A fifth ring. Don't risk it! But her hand seemed to have a life of its own.

"Hello?"

"Chels, it's me, Amber. Listen, I'm all set here, and I was wondering if you'd like me to help you pack. Chelsea? Are you there? Answer me!"

"He called."

"What?"

"The man. He called. Here."

"Oh, my God! Call the police!" Amber ordered. "Chelsea, do it *now*!"

"I did. They don't believe me."

"Why not? Are they crazy? Get out of there, Chelsea! No! Wait! Hold on, and I'll come get you! You can follow me back in your car. Okay?"

"The man said no one would believe me, and he was right. He told me to stay out of Smythe Towers. He said I've made trouble for him. Trouble for *him*, and he's framed my father!" Chelsea started to shake violently.

"I'm scared for you, Chelsea. What if he's right outside your house with one of those hand-held phones? You're not safe!"

"Amber, listen to me. I'm going into the Towers. Right now. Tonight."

Silence. Amber couldn't seem to take in what she'd just heard.

"He's afraid I'll find something. He wouldn't have called me unless he was afraid. The police will come tomorrow and seal everything off. I won't be able to get inside, and I need to look through—there's got to be something there. I'll never get a chance to get in there if I don't go now."

"Where? What are you talking about? The Communication Room?

"No." She swallowed, trying to ease the tension in her throat. "I want to go to Diane's office. The key to it was one of the ones we copied. I still have the duplicates."

She could hear Amber breathing over the phone. Or was that her own breath, in and out? Chelsea's head throbbed.

Finally, Amber broke through the silence. "I'm coming with you." Her voice was deliberate.

"No—"

"Yes. Listen to me, Chelsea. We've gone a long way. Together. I want to do this. A man in Smythe Towers killed Diane. He's terrifying you, he's set up your dad, and he's going to walk away, scot-free. Well, not if I have anything to say about it."

"Amber, it's dangerous—"

"I'll come by and get you. I'll tell my parents that I'm helping you pack, and then . . . we'll do it."

"You're sure?"

"Yes. Ten minutes," Amber said. "Be ready."

14

Amber pulled the parking stub from the machine. The two of them watched as the metal arm glided up, silently granting them entrance.

"Where do you want me to go?" Amber asked.

"Go right to the Communication Room door. My key opens the basement elevator lobby."

Inside the garage, the night seemed perfectly still, as if the tide of cars had swept out for the evening and the rhythm had stopped; the cycle wouldn't begin again until Monday. Overhead, the cement dome of the garage held the exhaust close, and the air tasted like metal in Chelsea's mouth. The parking garage was empty. Eleven o'clock on a Friday evening, and everyone had scurried from Smythe Towers for their weekend celebrations.

"Down that ramp, right?" Amber asked, pointing.

Chelsea nodded. They snaked their way to the basement parking lot. Easing into a space, Amber turned off the lights and cut the engine. They both sat, staring out the windshield into gray concrete wall.

During the ride over, she and Amber had barely spoken. While Amber drove, Chelsea's mind had gone off on bizarre twists and turns. She'd seen couples clinging to each other, laughing, kissing, and she'd become suddenly angry. Angry that the lives of those people were untouched, that they could drift through this blissful summer's evening smiling absurdly, still believing that the world was a safe and happy place. She'd had the urge to get out and shake them; she'd wanted to place her face so close their lips would almost touch, and she wanted to scream, "Don't be so stupid! Our world is a horrible place! People lie all the time! People kill!"

"You realize he might be in there," Chelsea said quietly.

"I know. But then again, he might not. He's probably at his home."

"We're walking blind, Amber. I think, I *know*, we're taking a risk."

"We'll go in and out. Like spies. And we'll get some answers. This guy was counting on scaring you. He wants you to play his game, his way. We've got to figure out what he's afraid of."

Reaching into her purse, Chelsea pulled up a small black cylinder encased in a leather sheath. "Mace," she said softly. "I don't want to go in there completely unarmed."

"Good. Before I left my house, I was thinking the same thing. Look what I brought." Amber drew a two-inch pocketknife from underneath the seat of her car and held it in her palm for Chelsea to see. It was red, with a tiny silver cross at its center.

Snorting, Chelsea said, "What are you going to do with that thing? Trim his nails?"

"It's the only knife I had." Amber watched her, wide-eyed. A grin flicked at the edge of her mouth. "Come on, Chels. *Trim his nails!?!* It's not *that* bad."

"That's a pathetic knife. A poor excuse—I don't

think it can even be technically called a knife!"

The absurdity of the picture hit her. Of the man, standing scared in the light of that paltry knife. Why was it so funny? She began to giggle.

"Wait! What's so funny? I've seen smaller knives," Amber protested.

"I think Barbie had a smaller one. Safari Barbie— little plastic thing—" They were both laughing now.

"I could hurt him—"

"His feelings, maybe."

Deep rose blotches formed on Amber's cheeks as she began to laugh, hard. Tears blurred Chelsea's vision, and she laughed until her sides ached and she was afraid she couldn't stop. They were convulsing in great, heaving gulps.

Amber smacked the steering wheel with her palm. "Stop it!" Amber gasped. "Stop! Stop! Stop!"

"I know. I think we're losing it!"

They finally slowed down. Chelsea rubbed her eyes. Amber wiped underneath her nose with a tissue she'd produced from the pocket of her jacket, and then she hiccupped.

"You're a good friend, Chelsea," Amber said. She

draped her arm around her and gave her a sideways hug.

"No, I'm not. If I were a good friend, I'd never let you go with me in there." She meant it. A true friend wouldn't lead someone she loved into danger. But even knowing that, Chelsea was glad she was not alone.

Amber sighed, and they sat for a moment in comfortable silence. She rested her head against the back seat and stared up at the ceiling. "You're the one who's a good friend. I feel really guilty."

"Guilty? Why?"

"Because I said all of that bad stuff about Diane." Giving Chelsea a quick glance, she added, "She was murdered, and I trashed her. I don't know why. I know you shouldn't say bad things about the dead. I'm sorry I said all of that stuff about her."

"You want to know what I think?"

"What?"

"I bet, deep down, you think that people who get killed deserve it."

"That's not how I—" Amber began.

Holding up her hand, Chelsea cut her off. "Let me finish. You want to find who killed Diane and all of that, but you also want to believe that only bad people are murdered. But now, who knows? We're good, and tonight it might be us. Am I right?"

"Maybe," Amber murmured.

"I think bad stuff gets spread around. The good and the bad get nailed every day. It's just the way it is."

"I guess you're right. But I still want to do this."

"Me too."

And then, responding to a cue they both felt, they stepped out of the car.

Chelsea fumbled through the keys, found the right one, and unlocked the door to the lobby. Inside were three elevator doors. She chose the middle one, and punched the button.

"Are you scared?" Chelsea asked.

"Yes."

"Me too."

The elevator doors slid open and they stepped inside. In silence, they watched the numbers change. Eighteen, nineteen, twenty, twenty-one . . . twenty-two. The doors opened, and the two of them stepped into the empty hallway.

The keys felt sweaty in Chelsea's hands. Every office they passed was shut, closed and dark. No strip of light coming out from underneath the doors. Just quiet, dead, then a door marked DIANE HUTTON SMYTHE, ATTORNEY-AT-LAW. Chelsea pushed in the key. The lock clicked, and they were inside.

Flipping on the light, Chelsea turned and stared. She wasn't prepared for the flood of memories that washed over her. Diane's plants. A picture of Diane and Chelsea hanging on the wall. The mahogany desk. The burgundy chairs. The faintest smell of Diane's perfume. Emotions choked her, but she pushed them aside.

"Are you okay?"

"I'm fine," Chelsea whispered. "Let's start at the desk."

Dropping the keys on the desktop, she scanned the stack of papers while Amber flipped through letters.

"Try to keep everything the same way," Chelsea said. "I don't want anyone to know we were here."

"What kind of law did she practice? Criminal?"

"No, it was with insurance mostly. Nothing sinister in that."

Chelsea carefully pulled open the desk drawer. Pens rolled in their slots. Gold paper clips, an engraved perfume dispenser. And then she saw something. Her mother's rose-engraved silver cigarette lighter. Carefully, Chelsea picked it up. Snapping open the lid, she let her thumb flick it on and the flame shot up, quick and hot, like the tongue of a snake.

"Did you find something?" Amber asked.

"My mother's lighter."

"I didn't know Diane smoked."

"Not *Diane,*" Chelsea flared. "My *mother,* Suzonne. Diane must have just taken it, like she did everything else. She didn't ask for anything, she just barged ahead and took, *stole*—" Chelsea choked on her words. Why did it matter? An insignificant cigarette lighter that Diane had probably taken to offer a light to her smoking clients. It was stupid to worry about it, but, then, it was like a snapshot of everything Diane did. Diane had felt entitled to pillage anything she'd wanted from their lives. From *her* life. Amber was right—she really was a taker.

"It's all right," Amber said, soothingly. "It's yours

now. We need to keep looking, Chels. I don't think we should stay here very long."

Chelsea shoved the lighter into her jeans pocket. She pulled the drawer open wider, carefully removing two yellow legal pads of lined paper. Underneath, she found an accordion-pleated folder, stuffed with twenty sheets of paper. Strange, it wasn't filed in the cabinet with all the others. She opened the folder and began to read.

Amber was combing through the contents of one file drawer, then another. "I can't see anything, Chelsea. Forms, papers, I don't know what we're looking for."

"Anything that will lead us to that man. . . . Wait a minute. What *are* these?"

Amber came to the desk and read over Chelsea's shoulder. "Insurance forms," Amber said. "She seems to have a lot of them. They're nothing—just reports on car accidents."

"But, look whose name is on every one of these forms. Kenneth Marcroft, M.D. His office is on the first floor of Smythe Towers. Look—he's the doctor on every single one of these claims."

"Really? He's *my* doctor, too. Well, I went to him

216

once. A while back." She flushed, then added, "I heard you could get a shot to help you lose weight. Dr. Marcroft was really nice, but he said I didn't need it and to go home."

"Do you remember his voice? Was he the one on the phone?"

"I don't know. Maybe if I heard him again—I just don't know. But I can't believe it would be him. No." She shook her head. "No way."

"Okay. Let's keep going." Chelsea felt a pulse of excitement. Pulling the top form, she read the name. "Venturos, Juan. See those cabinets over there? Check in the file under V and see if you can find a corresponding file."

Stepping to the corner of the room, Amber pulled open the drawer of a cherry wood file cabinet. With her forefinger, she raked the tops until she stopped at a tab. "Got it," Amber said, waving a file in the air.

"What's it say?"

She leafed through a sheaf of papers until she came to the last sheet. Frowning, she scanned the page.

"It says Juan Venturos was involved in a car accident. He was rear-ended, and was injured. His injuries included a broken arm, fractured skull, whiplash, and permanent paralysis in his left hand. He won a damage claim of"—Amber's eyes widened—"four hundred thousand dollars. The man that rear-ended Juan Venturos had to pay out four hundred thousand dollars."

"Who was Juan insured with?"

Flipping back through more sheets of paper, Amber finally said, "Journeymen's Mutual. Diane was Juan's attorney. They sued Journeymen's Mutual, who paid out. Big time."

"Try Debra Gold. See if there's a file."

The second drawer opened with a bang. Amber rifled through, then pulled out another thick file.

"Gold, Debra." It was stuffy in the office, and beads of sweat had gathered along the edges of Amber's face. "Debra was in a car accident. Rear-ended. She suffered whiplash, a broken leg, crushed vertebrae. For her injuries, she won a three hundred thousand–dollar settlement from the driver of the other vehicle. The driver of the car that hit Debra was insured with Continental Insurance Company. The doctor was . . . Kenneth Marcroft, M.D." Amber gave a little gasp. "This doesn't make any sense. He's a *diet* doctor. I mean, he's an M.D., but these are heavy-duty injuries."

"Look up Anthony Wingate."

"Three hundred twenty-five thousand dollars in a court settlement against the driver of the other car. He was rear-ended! Injuries included whiplash, a bruised kidney, crushed pelvis, and a broken arm. Insured by . . . Sentry Insurance. Attending physician . . . Dr. Kenneth Marcroft."

"Look at this accident form. Look!" Chelsea held up a half-filled page. "Amber, Dr. Kenneth Marcroft has already signed the form, but . . . nothing's written in!"

One by one, they made their way through the papers. Each one in Chelsea's hand had a thick corresponding file in the cabinet. Chelsea would call the name, Amber would find it and drop it on a credenza by the file cabinet. Together, they worked, intent, not looking up until the last one had been found. Chelsea stared at the thick stack by Amber's hand. She was flushed. The information flowed through her, connecting in a perfect pattern.

"This Dr. Marcroft and Diane—they must have

been doing some kind of fraud," she told Amber. *"That's* where she got her money! Diane was involved in a scam, and these forms prove it!"

The door to Diane's office swung open.

"Indeed, they do, Chelsea," a man said. He was holding a gun, pointing it right at Chelsea's chest.

And then he smiled.

15

The man stepped through the door and shut it quietly behind him. He held a briefcase in his left hand, a small silver gun in his right.

"I'm sure you can guess who I am."

Chelsea stared at the gun. "Dr. Marcroft?"

His smile curled at the edges. "A pleasure to meet you. You're Chelsea, and you're"—he pointed the gun at Amber—"Amber Farrington. Do you remember me?"

Chelsea and Amber stared, frozen. Dr. Marcroft was close to fifty, with gently waving white hair and eyes the color of faded denim. His hands, his entire person, seemed pale; his body was thin, his voice soothing. If it weren't for the gun, Chelsea would have thought him the perfect picture of a physician.

"Well, never mind. I suppose I can't expect your manners to be too good, under the circumstances. Now, I want you to do exactly as I say. If you do, I promise, I won't hurt you. Understood?" He took a quick inventory of the room, looking at the folders, at their purses. "Amber," he said, his voice smooth, "we'll begin with you. Pick up your purse and put it in the corner. Chelsea, do the same with yours, then go stand beside her."

Chelsea rose from behind Diane's desk, slowly. The Mace, the knife, every chance at defense had been tucked safely inside their purses. What had they been thinking? What good was a weapon, any weapon, left inside a bag? Stupid! There was nothing they could do now. First Amber, then Chelsea did as he said, dropping their purses in a small heap five feet from Marcroft's feet, so close she could smell his cologne. Chelsea stood at the wall next to Amber, so that their shoulders barely touched.

He reached down and flipped open his wine-colored leather briefcase. "Chelsea, I believe I need that folder you were playing with. I'd like you to set it inside my briefcase." The gun made a slicing motion through the air. "Now."

Chelsea went to the desk and picked up the folder.

"Don't try to be cute, Chelsea. I want all of them. Just set them in the briefcase. That's the way. Fortunately, Diane kept all of our active cases in the same spot. I don't want too many questions if the police search her office, which I'm sure they will first thing tomorrow."

He grinned again.

"Don't look so surprised, Chelsea. I've got a patient who works in the police department. I know all about everything." He gave a thin smile. "It's called networking. After I read the newspaper article, I called my patient. He was more than willing to tell me what had happened. Stand back, Chelsea," he said, waving her toward the wall.

His eyes settled on Amber.

"I'm sorry we have to meet again under these circumstances. Bring me the stack of files on the credenza. Good girl. Do exactly as Chelsea did, and set them inside my briefcase. Perfect!" he said. "You follow orders very well. Please, go stand back beside your friend. That's the way." He squatted down, snapped the briefcase shut. Standing, he said, "I knew Diane and I had left a paper trail. But I think this should just about do it. Thank you both for your cooperation."

They watched each other. To Chelsea, the warmth of Marcroft's face was confusing; his smile, the soft notes of his voice promised that everything would be okay. But the gun was kept steady, and one small squeeze of the trigger would mean death.

"Now, here's what we're going to do. We're going to take a little walk down into the Communication Room. Chelsea, you need to understand that there will be a gun, right in Amber's back. If you move, run, scream, do anything at all, I'll shoot her, and then you. Understood?"

"Why did you kill Diane?" Even though her heart raced in her chest, Chelsea's voice sounded strangely calm. In a way, she didn't seem involved with her speech; she was standing back, watching the scene as if it were a play.

"Kill Diane?" He shook his head. "Do you see what eavesdropping does? It gives you all kinds of false impressions. I'm a *doctor*. I don't *kill* people. Her death was an accident. An unfortunate, unforeseen accident. We've been doing this a long time, and no one's ever been hurt before." Shaking his head, he murmured, "What bad luck!"

"If it was an accident, then why did you dump her body?" Chelsea cried. "Why did you have to weigh her down and throw her in a lake?"

"It's obvious you've figured out part of the picture. Diane and I are—*were*—in a partnership. A very lucrative partnership. We made an unholy trinity: Diane, myself, and a 'friend.' I believe you heard Pete on the phone?" He looked at her face, nodding. "That's what I thought."

"Then Pete killed her."

"Chelsea, you're not listening to me. No one killed her. It was just a setup gone sour. Pete staged car accidents. I filled out the forms that proved the passengers riding in the rear-ended cars were seriously injured, which, of course, they weren't. Diane filed those lawsuits," he said, pointing to the briefcase at his feet. "The insurance money came to Diane. Between us we split an incredible fortune. Unhappily, your father found Diane's bank statement and became suspicious. He told Diane she had to leave, and Diane decided to go to Texas and set up her own ring. She went riding with Pete yesterday so she could study the operation. He'd picked a target up Mullhollow Canyon. They swooped in front of the Jeep, slammed the brakes . . . but"—he made a sharp sound between his lips—"instead of it being a little fender bender, the Jeep hit Pete's car hard. The force sent their vehicle crashing broadside into a boulder. Diane was killed. Fortunately, Pete was still able to drive the car away. He kept driving up the canyon, trying to figure out his next move until he ended up at Dover Cave."

"So it was Pete, calling you, telling you about the 'complication,'" Chelsea whispered. She shuddered, picturing Diane smashed in the car, and Pete pulling her out and leaving her in the cave. "The complication was that Diane had been accidentally killed."

"Exactly."

"And Pete wanted to take her cut?"

"Ridiculous, wasn't it, when you consider there wouldn't be a claim filed on that one? But Pete can be greedy." He stroked the barrel of the gun with his index finger, almost as if he were petting it. "I was appalled when he took off Diane's diamond earrings before dumping her body into Dover Lake. When he told me he'd taken those earrings, I was furious. I said, 'Pete, you are a ghoul!' But I must say, it's a lucky thing for me that Pete is so rapacious." He looked at Chelsea, his eyes glinting hard. "Those earrings came in quite handy, don't you think?"

"So then it was—?"

"We've done enough talking." His hand shot up. "The rest is none of your concern."

"But just tell me—"

"It's none of your business. In fact, if your father had taught you how impolite it was to snoop, none of these unfortunate consequences would have to happen now. I can't tell you how upset I was when I realized you'd listened in on *me*, on my private conversation." He narrowed his eyes and raised the gun. His fingers squeezed the pistol grip. "Whatever happens now, as far as I'm concerned, the fault is yours."

Chelsea tried to ignore her terror. Would he let them live? No! she answered herself. They knew too much. It was over for her and Amber. It didn't matter how much he smiled. They were going to die.

Head erect, he bent down and grasped the handle of his briefcase. "Let's get on with it. It's time to take a little walk. Chelsea, take the keys off the desk. Let's go." With his gun, he motioned Chelsea and Amber to walk ahead of him. As Amber stepped by, he grabbed her close and stabbed the gun into the small of her back.

"Okay, Chelsea, open the door. There shouldn't be anyone around, but just in case, I want you to look happy. Come on, girls, smile! Are you ready? Three happy friends, taking a little walk. Go!"

They stepped into the hallway.

"Now, let's take a ride to the basement," Marcroft hissed.

The hallway was empty, silent, except for the rhythm of their footsteps as they walked to the elevators. Should she scream? Then Amber would take a bullet. And who would hear? Whoever came into Smythe Towers at midnight? Chelsea swallowed, and punched the elevator button. *Please, let someone be inside the elevator! Please! Let there be someone, working late!* But when the door slid open, the elevator was empty.

Amber began to shake. But she didn't make a sound during the entire, endless elevator ride. When the doors glided open, Amber's knees buckled, but Marcroft jabbed the gun deeper into her back.

"We can end this now. Is that what you'd like?"

"I'm okay," Amber whispered.

The three of them moved forward in a tight knot until they were in the parking garage. But instead of walking directly to the Communication Room, Marcroft directed them to a spigot on the wall opposite the Communication Room door. He reached down and turned it on full blast. A sputter, then a violent stream of water shot straight out of the end of the hose and washed down the cement floor.

"Now, ladies, we're ready for the Communication Room. Move it!"

They walked in the water's path. In just a few moments, the cold water seeped through Chelsea's shoes, soaking her feet. Water coated the garage floor until it shone like a black pearl. Amber slipped, and Chelsea grabbed her elbow to steady her.

"Open the door!" Marcroft ordered. He set the hose down so that the water streamed away from the doorway, then placed his briefcase against the wall, out of the water's path. "I *said,* open the door. Now!"

Chelsea glanced around.

"There's no one here. I'll tell you one more time, Chelsea. Open that door, or we'll end it here."

With shaking fingers, Chelsea unlocked the door and the three of them stepped inside.

"Get onto the platform. Over by the goat. Come on, ladies. You'll be fine!"

They hesitated. Marcroft cocked his gun. "It's up to you."

Amber stepped awkwardly onto the platform. Chelsea followed and stood beside her.

"All the way back, ladies. Next to the panel over there. Put the keys on the desk, by the computer. Good, good. Now, pick up the goat. Plug it in."

The machines droned on.

"What are you doing?" Amber cried in terror. "What are you doing? What are you doing?"

"It's just going to be another devastating accident. It will be obvious to even the densest detective what happened here. You were back in Smythe Towers, trying to build a case to save Mr. John Smythe. You even broke into Diane's office. The police will find your purses, and then will discover your prints all through her things. You came into the Communication Room. Tragically, the maintenance man left the water running after his typical Friday cleaning. But you two didn't understand the danger you were in. You were too busy tinkering with the computer. Sit down, Chelsea. I want you to look like you're typing."

"No."

"Suit yourself," he said. He cocked the gun and aimed the barrel at Amber's middle.

Chelsea set her hands on the keyboard.

"Go and get a chair, Amber. Now, wheel it next to Chelsea. Pretend you're staring intently at the screen. You know, the information you gave me about the phone records was crucial. I never would have thought of interoffice calls as being traceable. Never. You two are very bright. I must say, I was truly impressed. But when I understood what you were doing, I had to get you out of there before you printed a hard copy. That would have shown my number linked to Diane's again and again and again." He shook his head. "If you girls could do it, then the police could, too. No, I've made close to four million dollars off of this little scheme. I'm not about to leave any evidence now. The Communication Room is in for a cataclysmic mishap, and you two are going to be caught in it."

He kicked a sandbag away, then another. Opening the door, he crouched and grasped the hose and brought it inside the Communication Room, so that the water arched over the sandbags and splashed against the platform. The ring of sandbags, created to keep water from the machines, now kept the water from Marcroft. Slowly, the door shut, resting against the thickness of the hose.

"Stop!" Chelsea screamed.

Marcroft talked louder to be heard over the spray of the water. "I'm sorry you had to come here tonight. I called you to make sure you'd stay away, but you didn't. I should have known you'd come. Diane told me you were a fighter. We talked about you, and how your mind worked. She loved you! She thought you were wonderful, sharp, beautiful, just like her. She was grooming you. You were going to be the next Diane."

"I don't understand what you're doing!" Amber screamed. "Why?"

But he seemed to focus only on Chelsea. His eyes never wavered from her face.

"Don't worry, Chelsea. It will be fast. It shouldn't hurt at all."

"What? What shouldn't hurt? You said you wouldn't hurt us!" Amber was sobbing now.

"I lied."

Amber, whimpering, pleading, didn't understand the way Chelsea did. Underneath the platform was a sea of wires pumping hundreds of thousands of volts of electricity. Water began to pool against the platform. An accident. An accident with enough electricity to crash the system and wipe out every phone record.

An accident that would electrocute Amber and Chelsea.

She couldn't die like this! This—man—holding a gun, couldn't just snuff out their lives! She had nothing, no way to fight! She'd have to think! Think!

The sound of the machines, pulsing, the water, spurting and splashing and leaking into the wires; what did she have to fight with?

The lighter felt hard in her pocket.

The lighter.

Fire.

A memory—what? What had Nola told her when she'd shown her the room? She glanced overhead. The room's machines were electrical. In case of a fire the sprinklers shot—foam! Foam that sucked the oxygen from the air, to keep electrical fires from spreading.

Marcroft's eyes were on the water rising behind the sandbags.

"Amber, hold your breath," Chelsea whispered. "When I say 'Now,' take a deep breath and hold it!"

"Shut up. Both of you."

Small crackling sounds came from underneath the platform. The water on the floor had pooled to more than an inch, seeping under the platform and into the wires. The crackling turned into a series of sharp pops. Sparks began to shoot in buzzing blue flashes. His eyes were on the water, on the sparks.

"All right, ladies. It's almost over." With a quick motion, Marcroft jerked open the door and threw out the hose. In that split second, Chelsea's hand dived into her pocket, yanked out the lighter, flipped open the lid. She stood.

Marcroft turned. His eyes snapped onto hers.

"What—?" He drew up his gun and aimed.

Knowing she was exposing her whole body to a bullet, Chelsea quickly reached the lighter high overhead.

"Sit down!" Marcroft roared. "I said *sit!*"

Chelsea flicked the lighter; the flame licked the sensor. A shot exploded from the gun, then a second, the bullets whizzing past her; a bell shrieked.

"Now!" Chelsea screamed. She took a deep breath the instant before the room shot full of white foam. Everywhere, like a thick, all-encompassing blizzard. It rained down, sucking all the oxygen from the room, from Marcroft's lungs. He dropped to his knees, foam encasing him in a shroud. He made hoarse, raking gasps. Grabbing Amber's hand, Chelsea yanked her forward; they slipped, righted themselves, pushed through the blinding foam, holding the air they'd trapped inside their lungs. They were off the platform now; Marcroft was hacking, spitting chunks of foam while his hand frantically groped for his gun, buried under the blanket of white. Chelsea could see his hand touch a flash of metal. He drew up the gun. And then, with everything she had, Chelsea kicked him hard in his soft underbelly.

He grunted and fell over the sandbags and onto his elbows, his face resting in water, and Chelsea kicked him again, and again, until Amber yanked her and they were out the door, running, coughing, sucking in air.

"Run!" Chelsea croaked.

The bell still screeched, covering the sound of their footsteps as they ran. Five steps. Ten. An electrical flash of blue shot from the doorway, followed by an earsplitting explosion and a blast of white light, and then utter darkness.

"Oh, my God," Amber cried. "Oh, my God, oh, my God!"

"I'm here," Chelsea said. "We're okay. It knocked the power out."

"The keys—to my car—they're in—Diane's office—"

"We're fine. We'll walk. Hold on to me. I've got my hand against the wall. Follow me, I know the way."

It wasn't long before sirens pierced the air, and for the first time in Chelsea's life, their wail sounded like church bells. Clutching on to each other, slipping, stumbling, they made their way up the ramp and out into the fresh air of the night.

16

Fayette tapped a pencil against its edge like a drumstick while his eyes moved from Chelsea, to her father, to Amber, then back to Chelsea.

"Well. You three have had quite a ride," he began. "I'm sure you're relieved it's finally over. Marcroft played mind games with you all. And especially with you, Chelsea. Diane had explained enough about the inner workings of Smythe Towers to really jerk you around. Do you know how he managed to send you that message right when Amber walked out of the room?"

"I don't know," Chelsea began.

Her father reached over and put his hand on top of Chelsea's. "I should have thought of it at the time, Chelsea. But, I arrived at the police station just when they found Diane's body and . . . I just couldn't pull it all together. The Communication Room has a special monitor with a microphone built in. Anyone who knows the access code can call the monitor from any telephone and listen in."

"I don't understand. . . ."

"It's a safety feature. The equipment in the Communication Room had a lot of warning buzzers. Nola would phone in and check the monitor every hour or so."

"Marcroft was listening in on us? On our conversation?" Chelsea felt herself shiver.

Fayette broke in. "I'm afraid so. We found the access number in his office. Apparently he was monitoring the Communication Room from his speakerphone. But the reason I called you all here is to inform you that we picked up the third man this morning. A Peter Karsch. Among a long list of crimes"—Fayette took a breath— "Karsch is being charged with Diane's murder."

"Murder?" Chelsea gasped. "Then he *did* kill Diane." She looked over at Amber, her eyes wide.

"No. That is not correct." Fayette leaned back in his seat and tossed the pencil onto a pile of papers. "Diane was killed accidentally, just the way Marcroft told you. The coroner's report supports his version of what happened in the car Karsch was driving. The irony was that Diane had never before gone along on one of the setups. First time. Normally, Karsch's girlfriend was the passenger, but Diane wanted to learn the ropes on the driving end so she could set up shop in another state."

"But *murder*?" Diane's father stared hard.

"In this type of case, it's the law. That's what Marcroft knew. *That's* what he was afraid of." He pointed straight at her father. "One thing's for sure. Had he lived, Dr. Kenneth Marcroft would have been tried for Diane's murder, right alongside Karsch."

Chelsea's father shook his head. He was dressed in khaki slacks and a cream knit shirt. In the two days since his release from jail, he hadn't worn a suit, even when he'd gone to Smythe Towers to survey the damage.

"I still don't understand. If it was an accident . . ."

"In any death that occurs while a crime is being committed, the charge is murder for every single one of the players, all the way to the top. Marcroft was a player. His butt would have fried." Fayette leaned back in his seat. He pulled his coffee mug toward him and lifted it for a sip, but stopped in midair.

"Did anyone tell you how much money was involved in this little scam of theirs?"

Chelsea cleared her throat. "Marcroft said he got a couple million—"

"Four million," Amber corrected. "He said he'd made four million dollars."

"Yeah?" Fayette snorted. "Well, the grand total was closer to nine million."

"Nine *million*!" her father gasped.

"You saw only one of Diane's checkbooks. This scam was some piece of work. The sad part is, it's hardly original. It's being done all over the country."

"My God," Chelsea's father breathed.

Fayette shook his head. "I'll tell you, I've learned a lot about this sting. Diane, Karsch, and Marcroft were just one small outfit. This accident insurance scam is a sixteen-billion-dollar-a-year industry, right now." He tapped his cup against the desk for emphasis. "It was a perfect scheme. Karsch would buy an old beat-up car. He'd find a nice, spanking-new automobile, the kind with lots of insurance, pass in front of it real close, and then wham! He'd slam on his brakes. The poor sucker behind him would go right up his tailpipe. Karsch and his passengers would get the insurance information from the victim. Enter Marcroft. He'd fake nasty injuries for Karsch and company and put them on insurance forms. Enter Diane. She'd take those fake forms with the fake names and sue the insurance companies. Big money. Karsch averaged twenty thousand dollars a month. Not bad for a kid with no high school education. Marcroft and Diane split the rest."

Chelsea's father rubbed his chin with his hand. "I had no idea," he murmured. "No idea."

Fayette nodded. "We realize that. I'll need just a little more information from you. Chelsea, Amber, you can step outside if you'd like. Mr. Smythe will be right out."

Chelsea and Amber rose from their chairs.

"I hope I don't see either one of you again," he said,

grinning slyly. "Nothing personal, you understand."

"Nothing personal, but we feel the same way," Chelsea replied. She smiled.

"Stay off that goat thing. You hear?"

"I swear, I'm done. When I get the urge, I'll pick up a *National Enquirer.*" Then, to her father, she said, "We'll be waiting out front, Daddy."

"Fine. I'll join you as soon as I'm finished."

The sun beat down on Chelsea's head as she and Amber settled into the bench in front of the station. The seat burned her thighs; the sun blazed along her scalp and the tops of her shoulders, but the sensation felt good. Amber shifted in the bench and squinted as the traffic rumbled by.

"Well. I'm glad they caught that guy," Amber said. "But I'm sorry Diane was involved."

"I guess you were right about her," Chelsea said softly.

"You were right about Marcroft. I thought he was so *nice.* I hardly knew him, but I couldn't believe something bad about my doctor. It must have been really hard to hear those things about Diane."

A woman in a dark suit hurried by, followed by a

teenage boy on Rollerblades. A man in a pair of jeans and a ponytail glanced at his watch, then crossed the street, muttering. Chelsea slid down the bench, so that her legs touched the curb and her head rested on the top rung of the bench. Closing her eyes, she thought of Diane, of all the things she'd learned about her and her father and herself in the past few days. Knowing what Diane had done gave her the same feeling she'd had when the police told her the cave was empty; she couldn't trust what she saw, couldn't believe what she felt. How could she have been so wrong?

"Are you okay?"

Shrugging, Chelsea said, "I don't know. Everything about Diane is so . . . confusing. I know what she did was immoral. It was terrible, and part of me hates her for it. But, I still . . ."

"Love her."

"Yes." She squinted up at Amber. "But that doesn't make any sense. I should despise her all the way, but . . ."

"You don't. And you know what?" Amber said quietly. "I think still caring for her is okay. I don't think you can just crack a person like an egg, and separate the white from the yolk and the good from the bad. It's all mixed together. She was good and bad. Love the good part, and deal with the rest."

"Have you always been this wise?"

"Always," Amber grinned. "You'd just forgotten."

Chelsea turned back to the street to watch the people hurry on their way. A woman clutched a small boy onto her hip while pulling a little girl in orange shorts behind her. A man who must have been the father carried two large shopping bags overflowing with brightly colored toys; a blue-and-white diaper bag banged against his hip. A man with a cellular phone hurried by, waving his free arm and yelling with every step. Normal people, normal lives.

"It's just, the thing that bothers me is that I let everything—everyone else slide. Diane took up the biggest part of my life, and now she's really gone. Both you and my dad said Diane changed my personality. . . ."

"Not all the way. You've always been bossy. You've always been a snoop. Diane didn't do that to you." Amber playfully punched her leg. "Those qualities are all yours. As for the rest of your personality disorders—no big deal. I'll help you get back to normal. And besides"—Amber's face turned suddenly serious—"in some ways, Diane changed you for the better. A year and a half ago, you would never have been tough enough to do what you did with the lighter. I was so scared, Chelsea. I couldn't do anything but stand there. But you looked as cool and tough as . . . as . . ."

"Diane."

"Yes. It saved our lives. I know it saved mine."

A shadow loomed over them both; Chelsea jumped as a hand rested lightly on the top of her head.

"Are you two ready?" her father asked.

"Oh!" Chelsea cried. "Dad. You scared me!"

With one hand, he pulled her to her feet. "We've really gone through it, haven't we? All of us," he said, moving around the bench to stand beside her.

"At least it's over," Chelsea said. "I was just sitting here thinking how much I want to get back to normal. I'm so glad it's finally over."

"No. I don't think it is. Not altogether."

With a start, Chelsea looked up into her father's face.

"Don't look so scared, Chelsea. I don't mean the

crime. What I mean is—when I was sitting in that jail, I had a lot of time to think. If things had gone . . . badly . . . for me, I wouldn't have missed Smythe Towers. I would have missed you. I've tried to handle our relationship like a business deal. That's what I know—business, the bottom line. I guess I thought I could order you to get close to me, but"—he spread his hands—"it seems daughters need a little more than that."

"I think fathers do, too," Chelsea told him.

Nodding slightly, he broke into a gentle smile.

It was time to go home.